S0-EFO-263

3998

splurch.com

12.1.1999 - 5.1.2000

BILL ALLARD

LAST GASP
of
San Francisco

MADE IT HAPPEN

David Allard
Margaret Allard
Kirk Knight
Dan Sokol

Copyright 2001 William D. Allard

World rights reserved. No part of this book may be reproduced or transmitted in any form or by any means, electronic or mechanical, including photocopy, recording, or by information storage and retrieval system, without the written permission of the Author, except for brief passages used in reviews of this book.

First Edition
2001

ISBN: 0-86719-535-5

This is a work of fiction. Any similarity to any person, place, or thing is unintentional and purely coincidental

01 02 03 04 05   5 4 3 2 1

Published and Distributed by Last Gasp of San Francisco
777 Florida Street
San Francisco, CA 94110
www.lastgasp.com

Book Design: Johanna Etc. Rudolph
Cover Art: Jonathan Sgro
Editors: Tiffany Maleshefski
              Laurent Martini

VISIT
www.splurch.com

TABLE OF CONTENTS

Splurchenous by Doctor Science

Splurchenous
BY
DR. SCIENCE

When I first read this book, I vomited. Could the scenes contained herein be true? Could the City that gave us Herb Caen have made like Esau and sold its birthright for a mess of hyped pottage?

The Internet is more than six zillion pre-pubescent webmasters gawking at sixty gazillion pictures of naked women, while six hundred gabillion annoying gif propelled icons sway back and forth in maddening repetition. It helps to think of the Internet as a vast Laundromat bulletin board, filled with postings from the sane and insane, the greedy and the needy. Many are out of date; referring to garage sales that happened last month and lost pets that were long ago found.

Interestingly enough, the word "Splurch" comes to us from the Indo-European "Splurchenous" which was an adjective describing that feeling you get when you're headachy and nauseous at the same time, ready to draw the blinds, lie down and breathe slowly, hoping the bad thoughts won't come again, the ones that tell you to throw the couch out the window and scream insults at Janet Reno, daring her to send the black helicopters and her legions of jack-booted thugs.

Today, Splurch can be a verb, an adjective, an adverb or a noun. "Let"s splurch him before he knows what hit him." "Wow, this new gum is really splurch!" "The runaway baby carriage bounced splurchily down the hill" or "His splurch lay on his tie like a miniature fried egg" All are good and delightful uses of this ancient word. Yet why did a dot com startup choose to call itself by this name?

I wish I could say it was simple ignorance, but the fact is, there is a devious intelligence at work here. Eyewitnesses claimed that Thomas Alva Edison's last words were "Splurch. Gumph. Flizbit." Fatally wounded by friendly fire, General Stonewall Jackson, gasped "Boys, let me splurch in the shade of the gum tree down by the swamp" Coincidence? I doubt it.

'Whatever inferences can be drawn from these facts, and I'm sure there are many, the undisputed fact remains that Splurch is a word which no spell checker recognizes, and by searching with the most sophisticated search engine of all, the Giant Halitosis Sponge, one comes up with only the web page promoting this book. Why the silence?

A quiet frog is a frightened frog. The wholesome croaking that celebrates a healthy pond is nowhere to be heard. Instead, we hear the ominous ticking the mantle clock; the pale specter of Vincent Price or someone like him muttering as he stirs the fire. Outside the ruined mansion, from the depths of the frog pond's murky water slowly surfaces a blood spattered board bearing the single word SPLURCH.

Here, in this tome the mystery unfolds, like a Venus fly trap opening her sticky pod to the unwary fly. Splurch on, gentle reader. We have nothing to fear but our own hype.

Dr. Science
The Fortress of Arrogance, July 2001

1999

126 Northern California companies launched IPOs

Average gain of their stock at the close of trading on December 31 was 358 percent.

MILENA

Wednesday * December 1, 1999
6:00 AM

"I am going to be soooooooo rich," sang Milena Peterson, Chief Executive Officer of splurch.com.

Splurch.com was going public, and when it did, all of Milena's dreams would come true.

"Freeeeeedom," she belted in her best Aretha Franklin. "Give me freeeeeeeeeedom."

She raced her Mercedes SLK through the light at 17th and down Bryant into the heart of San Francisco's exploding dot com community. It was 6 A.M., but the streets were already filled with bright eyed workers racing to get a jump on the competition.

Milena glanced at the bulging bag of Christmas decorations bouncing on her passenger seat. Decorating the office for the Wednesday company meeting was the perfect way to prepare the troops for today's announcements.

I am doing too much, Milena thought, as her headlights illuminated block after block of dilapidated warehouses, ancient auto parts stores, and billboards announcing the arrival of yet another indispensable dot com web site.

Steve Jobs wouldn't do this at Apple.

Milena pulled in front of the dirty yellow two-story brick building that was now the home of splurch.com.

"This is not too much," Milena whispered as she carried the bag of decorations towards the battered door with the cardboard taped to the window announcing www.splurch.com in blue magic marker. "It demonstrates my personal commitment to the splurch.com working environment."

splurch.com

Scott McNealy wouldn't do this at Sun.

Milena hung twinkling lights on row after row of computers, slapped a large digital Santa on the company refrigerator, and draped silver mylar Christmas wreaths on all the white boards in the programming and engineering department at the rear of the building.

Steve Balmer wouldn't do this at Microsoft.

The phone rang.

Milena raced up the red metal circular staircase to her loft command center. Only one person would be calling this early.

"Good morning Tom."

"Ready to announce the move?" asked Tom Samoley.

"I guess," sighed Milena. "Sure we want to do this?"

"Can't afford not to. Unfortunately, I won't be there when you make the announcement."

"You said you would be here," said Milena. "It's going to take a lot of hand holding and I only have two hands."

"You can do it," said Tom. "You're the best."

"And you're a jerk."

"Sorry. I over-scheduled my morning."

"I need you. I need a MAN to help me with this job," said Milena in the most sarcastic tone she could manage.

"Sure you do," laughed Tom. "But you're the Chief Executive Officer and I am just the acting Chief Financial Officer. Besides, you're more than a woman in my book."

"Okay Mr. Chicken, I'll handle it all by my lonesome," snapped Milena.

"You're the best," Tom said clicking off.

Tom Samoley is an asshole, Milena thought as she started putting dancing reindeer stickers on the computers. Tom was the lead splurch.com investor, and was always there when she announced good news but rarely around for the more controversial proclamations.

2

At 8:57 A.M., Milena started gathering her team. She marched through the office banging on a pot that she had pulled out of the bowels of the kitchen cabinet.

"Splurch.com weekly meeting is happening now. Attention all employees. This is your CEO Milena Peterson requesting the pleasure of your company at the bottom of the circular stairs."

Holly Chen, Milena's new associate producer, followed Milena singing a Christmas song that she and Salvidor Zaldivar, splurch.com's boy programming genius, had written the night before. The song focused on splurch.com employee work habits and was obviously composed after the consumption of more than a few cocktails.

Milena took a position half way up the circular staircase as happy employees gathered below her.

"Two major announcements," Milena began. "Our IPO is on target. We go public in four months,"

The room was engulfed in cheers.

"We have to move the office again," Milena announced as the celebration subsided.

"Somewhere off Third Street?" shouted Norman Dotoshay. Norm was an old hacker and the third employee hired by splurch.com. "That's where all the dot coms are moving."

"It's a little farther than that," said Milena.

The room got quiet.

"Where are we going?" asked Holly.

"Downtown San Jose," replied Milena.

An earthquake groan rolled through the room and exploded in one question.

"Why San Jose?"

TOM

$

Wednesday * December 1, 1999
12:17 AM

"He thought you would write him a check," laughed the man in the blue blazer.

"He thought you'd write a check right there at the meeting," screamed Tom Samoley as he gleefully pounded on the table under a large painting of "The Wreck of the Margaret Ann" at Buck's in Woodside.

"He thought that once we heard the idea, we would immediately write him a check. He would take the check home, deposit it in a bank in BumF__k, South Dakota, and start rolling in dot com dollars," giggled the man in the Armani suit across the table from Tom.

"It was that good an idea," announced the man in the checkered vest.

"THAT GOOD AN IDEA," all four men shouted. They all stood up, saluted, and crumpled back into their chairs in gales of laughter.

Tom loved these gatherings. It was the only time he spent with guys that weren't intimidated by his money or his position. All four were part of Tom's "Buck's Lunch Bunch" – a rotating group of friends and Silicon Valley investors types who got together to share investor war stories.

A man in a red bow tie raised his hand when the laughter died and said in his best fake announcer voice, "Now the continuing saga of The Wireless Wonder."

The group exploded in cheers.

"You remember last time," Bow Tie announced, "Wireless Wonder was running out of cash for the second time."

Tom grabbed a napkin, pinched the middle, and held it to his head like a little girl's bow. "Tell us again Mr. Announcer," Tom squeaked in his best falsetto, "what has happened in our adventure so far?"

4

"Who wants a recap of the action?" Bow Tie asked.

Everyone at the table banged on the tables and chanted, "recap, recap, recap."

"Wireless Wonder spent six years developing a new wireless device," explained Bow Tie. "Our heroic investor knew it would be a successful product because he always does such excellent what?"

Bow Tie pointed at Blue Blazer who had raised his hand.

"Due Diligence," said Blue Blazer.

"That's right," continued Bow Tie. "And our hero offered Wireless Wonder a million dollars for 70% of his company."

"Wireless was ecstatic... he had a million dollars," Checkered Vest laughed.

"And a market cap of just under 1.5 million," added Armani Suit.

"And somebody really smart to tell him how to spend the money," giggled Blue Blazer.

"Alas, the Wireless Wonder's million dollars.... ," announced Bow Tie.

"Disappeared just like that," said Tom snapping his fingers.

"Just like that," the whole group repeated and snapped.

"Correct," announced Bow Tie. "Now Wireless had no money and got scared. Our heroic investor told him *FEAR NOT! We'll increase the value of the shares to two dollars, and I'll buy 70% of your shares so we can keep this deal going.*"

"Pro Rata would be the magic term," announced Blue Blazer.

Checkered Vest stood up, pulled out an imaginary pad and pencil, and pretended to struggle with the math. "That would give our hero 91% of the company and Wireless 9%."

"But last week Wireless realized he was going to run out of money at the end of the month," said Bow Tie

"Owwwwwwww....." the whole table moaned..

"Poor Wireless," fake sobbed Armani Suit.

"Do not lament," barked Bow Tie. "Our hero offered to increase the share value to four dollars and purchase another 70%."

"Ho-ray," cheered the booth.

"How much of his company would Wireless Wonder now own?" wondered Bow Tie.

Vest again pulled out his imaginary pad and pencil set. "2.7%."

"Right," whispered Bow Tie, "but this morning Wireless decided he no longer wanted to run the company."

The booth sat in stunned silence.

"He's walking away?" asked Tom.

"That's right," smiled Bow Tie. "He wants me to help him find someone to run the business because I know what I am doing"

"You sure do," exclaimed Tom as he shook Bow Tie's hand.

"You're the best," said Checkered Vest shaking Bow Tie's other hand.

"The best," repeated the group in unison.

Shirley, their waitress, approached the table. "More coffee gentleman."

"Is it past noon?" asked Tom.

"Yes."

"Shall we have a real drink to celebrate this win?" Tom asked.

"I don't know about you fellows, but I want to make some more money this afternoon," announced Checkered Vest as he stood up. "No time to party."

Everybody agreed the alcohol could wait and started reaching for their wallets.

"I got it," said Tom as he threw a hundred dollar bill on the table.

"Heard you're taking splurch.com public," said Blue Blazer as he headed for the door.

"Gonna try."

"Let us know," said Armani Suit.

"Of course," said Tom as he threw another hundred dollar bill on the table and winked at Shirley. "Isn't that how it works?"

December 2, 1999

Equinox Gets $280 Million

Thursday * December 2, 1999
7:32 AM

"I AM NOT GOING!" shouted Sal Zaldivar as he raced down Arkansas and leaned into the turn at 17th. "I don't care how much money they throw at me."

Sal pedaled furiously and continued to shout into the wind. "San Jose sucks. I am not going to San Jose."

Sal took a right on DeHaro and pulled into Sally's, one of the shops in the corrugated blue metal fortress across from Abby's Party Rentals on 16th.

"Heard splurch.com is moving to San Jose," a tall bearded regular shouted as soon as Sal stepped into the bakery.

"Bye Sal," said his T-shirted friend.

"Bye Sal," sang a group of engineers standing next to the large refrigerator filled with Odwalla fruit juices. "Bye Bye Bye."

"I might not go," said Sal as he lined up for his morning jolt of caffeine.

"You're going," said Beard. "Sal Zaldivar has too much to lose if he isn't splurching when the splurch.com IPO hits the street."

"Money, isn't everything," Sal said.

"Not everything," laughed Beard, "but pretty damn close to everything."

T-shirt swayed in front of the off white wall sculpture covering the back wall of Sally's. "Is there anything money isn't?"

"When splurch.com goes public you'll be rolling in F.U. money," continued Beard, "there is no way you are going to give up that kind of dough by not moving to San Jose."

"We'll see," said Sal.

"About a month after the move, you'll be driving a car to work just like everybody in San Jose."

"And everybody in Los Angeles," shouted T-shirt.

All found the connection between driving to work in San Jose and Los Angeles hilarious. Sal decided to forgo his morning caffeine.

When Sal carried his bike through the splurch.com front door, Milena came bounding down the stairs from her executive office loft.

"Salvidor Zaldivar – just the man I need to talk to," she said cheerily.

"Is it about the Niners?" asked Sal.

"No, it isn't about the Niners," laughed Milena.

"Is it about Elvin Jones and Max Roach?" asked Sal.

"No, it isn't about the history of jazz drumming," laughed Milena even louder.

"Then it has to be sex."

"No it isn't about sex."

"That covers my areas of expertise," said Sal as he hoisted his bike on his shoulder and headed for his cubicle in the rear of the building.

"I need the best GUI designer in the Bay Area to help me figure out how we are going to make the colors on the new pages work," Milena said sweetly wrapping her arm around his shoulder and walking with him towards the back of the former auto parts warehouse.

"The colors look great," exclaimed Sal.

"They look great on your Mac but they have to look good for all users – including our PC friends," said Milena.

"Screw the PC people. If they really cared about color they'd use a Mac," Sal said as he hung his bike on pegs next to his desk.

"We've been through this before," said Milena patiently, "Most people have PCs. We have to keep them happy."

Milena and Sal spent the next hour trying different colors until they found a combination that worked for all computer users.

Sal thought about how much he liked working with Milena. She paid attention to detail and had a great sense of humor. It was going to be hard to tell her that he wasn't moving to San Jose with splurch.com.

"Milena," he finally stuttered.

Milena turned from the screen. "Yes, my computer genius," she said sweetly.

"I've been thinking about the move to San Jose."

"So have I. Next week I was planning to run down to San Jose with Holly and check out possible office spaces. You would be the perfect person to join us and help decide which space will work best for us."

"Is the move a done deal?"

"As soon as we find the right space it is," said Milena. "Is Wednesday good for you?"

"Norm and I are digitizing on Wednesday."

"Thursday?"

"I have practice on Thursday. I was planning to leave early."

"Then we'll go Friday. On the way back, we'll take 280 and stop by Tom Samoley's office on Sand Hill Road for Christmas drinks and see if he has any gold laying around he can throw our way."

Sal stared at his computer screen trying to figure out what to say next.

"A plan?" Milena asked as she patted Sal's shoulder.

"A plan," sighed Sal. "I guess."

NORM

Friday * December 3, 1999
10:42 AM

Norm dyed his hair. Not hot pink. Not electric blue. Not vomit green. He dyed it black. It was already dark. Now it was darker.

"You look different, Norm"

"New glasses?"

"Ya did something to your hair... right?"

Norm had thought about a tattoo. There was no way. When you're fifty-one you don't get tattoos. He considered a piercing. Just one of his ears. If he didn't like it, it would grow back. Right? Knowing his luck, it would get infected and he'd have to have his ear amputated.

Splurch.com had hired two more twenty-somethings last month so Norm dyed his hair. He had to keep this job. He had to pay the mortgage on his house in San Jose. When the splurch.com IPO hit he could pay it off. He just had to hang on 'til then.

"Got a minute, Norm?" Milena, leaned into his cubicle and radiated one of her two thousand watt smiles.

"Sure."

Norm clicked the keyboard and the stream racing across the screen froze instantly. "What can I do you out of?"

"There's a problem with the site, " Milena said as she casually parked herself on the corner of his desk.

"What kind of problem?"

"It's taking too long to download the home page. Tom Samoley just called. He tried to download the site and it took him so long he finally gave up."

Tom was the main man at Samoley Ventures – the only company with real money invested in splurch.com. If Tom Samoley was unhappy, then every splurch.com employee was unhappy.

Norm sighed and tried to think of where to start the problem solving.

"Which one of his computers was he using?"

"I don't know."

"If he tried to download from his palm pilot it won't work."

"That could have been it. He was in his Ferrari calling me from his cell phone. Why won't the site work on his palm?"

"Because the site is not formatted to work on a palm pilot."

"Well let's format it to work on a palm," said Milena. She leaped up and started pacing around Norm's tiny cubicle. "Everybody has palms. Maybe we can form a strategic alliance with a palm pilot company. I have a friend who just started a company is selling a new kind of wireless hand-held computer. I'll call her right now." Milena picked up Norm's gun phone and started to punch numbers on the holster.

"There's another problem," sighed Norm as he pulled down his browser and clicked to the splurch.com web site. He didn't want to get into a ridiculous discussion with Milena about the impossibility of formatting splurch.com for palm pilots and decided now was the perfect time to bring up the downloading problems with the new logo that Milena had forced Sal to add to the home page yesterday.

"What other problem," said Milena warily as she stopped punching numbers and put Norm's gun phone back into it's holster.

Holly Chen appeared at the cubicle doorway.

"Jack Brouchet just called. He said that you were supposed to be doing a conference call with him."

"Oh my God, that's right. Did he say when it was?" Milena screamed as she swept by Holly and headed back to her loft.

"He said it was supposed to start fifteen minutes ago."

"Ahhhhhhhh.....," Milena's scream echoed against the yellow brick office walls as she sprinted past cubicle after cubicle of startled

12

splurch.com employees.

Holly and Norm shared a grin. Norm liked Holly. She started at splurch.com a month ago but every time she saw Norm, she still gave him a big smile. She also didn't seem as full of herself as the other new child employees. Or as over-confident. Or as patronizing to the older computer geniuses like himself.

"I have to tell you something Norm," Holly whispered. She leaned back out into the cubicle corridor, looked both ways, and then put her head close to Norm's. Holly used some kind of shampoo that was the best smelling stuff in the world. It was making Norm crazy to be this close to her.

"What," Norm said as he took large gulps of air into his mouth so he wouldn't get any more brain damaging whiffs of hair.

"I saw a new organizational chart on Milena's desk this morning."

"What a surprise," laughed Norm, "they reorganize this company at least once a month. Sometimes twice"

"Your name wasn't on the list," Holly said.

"Are you sure," gasped Norm.

"I checked three times. Norman Dotoshay wasn't on the list – anywhere."

December 3, 1999

Stock of McAfee.com Triples

HOLLY

Friday * December 3, 1999
10:11 PM

A Tom Waits fan must have had a pocketful of quarters because "The Piano Has Been Drinking" had been playing all night long. Holly Chen wasn't upset. She liked Waits and the guy hitting on her had a cute butt.

"Dot com gal?"

"Yeah."

"Which one?"

"Splurch."

"Never heard of it."

"You will. We're going public in a couple of months."

"Cool." Mr. Cute Butt sipped his drink and wiggled a little closer.

"And we're doing billboards."

Butt reached for his wallet. "I am a designer. I do real cool work. Let me give you my card."

"Noooooo...." Holly finished her vodka tonic and climbed off the stool. "We're moving to San Jose and I have to go to the bathroom very badly."

Holly playfully punched her stunned pursuer and headed towards a door marked "BROADS." The boredom bell was ringing and when it rang this early in an encounter Holly knew it was time to retreat. The second "cool" did him in. If she never heard the word "cool" again, Holly would be a happier person.

What a horrible day, Holly thought, as she hovered over the porcelain throne.

14

This morning, three packed 38 Gearys had raced by her stop. When she was finally able to board a bus, she was forced to stand with her breasts smashing into a high school backpack every time the driver made another one of his explosive take offs.

As soon as Holly walked in the splurch.com front door, Milena grabbed a floppy disk off the receptionist's desk and waved it in her face.

"Holly, take this to the Kinko's. Print out a color copy of all the presentation files in the Brouchet Folder and make ten copies of each."

"Coffee," mumbled Holly as she stumbled in the general direction of the coffee pot, "I need caffeine."

"Holly, you're twenty minutes late. We need this done now."

Holly took the disk. "Okay. I'll try doing it with non-caffeinated brain waves. But you're chancing a possible Holly shut down. How do I get there?"

"That's right. You don't have a car." Milena crunched her face into executive thinking mode.

"Noooooo... car," Holly sighed as she tried to maneuver around Milena for another shot at the coffee pot.

Milena grabbed Holly's hand and slapped a key into it. "Take my Mercedes. It's in the first spot. I was here at 5:30 am."

"You must have an army of worms stored in your desk," laughed Holly as she headed for the door. Milena didn't hear the joke. She was already tackling another splurch.com crisis on the other side of the warehouse.

When Holly started the car, the wipers came on and she couldn't turn them off. Should she go back in and ask somebody for help? Too embarrassing.

Holly drove to Kinko's under sunny skies with the wipers going full blast. To drown out the dry squeak squeak squeak, she turned up LIVE 105 and sang along with every song as loud as she could.

Holly had a friend at Kinko's who helped her get the pages printed, but none of the color copiers were working so Holly returned to splurch.com without making any copies, and Milena was forced to pass around individual color prints at her meeting.

*You should have gone to the Kinko's on Van Ness to get the copies made," Milena said after the meeting.

"I wanted to make it back in time for your presentation."

"You could have made it," said Milena as she started up the circular stairs. "Remember, we're a team. We'll both be stockholders in a couple of months."

"But one of us will have a mountain of stock and one of us will have a small pile of shares that can't be turned into real money for a long time," Holly muttered.

"What?"

"GO SPLURCH," Holly yelled as she raised both her arms and started doing a splurch.com version of one of her most popular high school football cheers.

The whole office joined in the cheer – even Milena.

"How many times is that going to work," Holly muttered to herself as she walked up Clement towards her apartment on Fourth.

"Holly Chen?"

Holly spun around. She was face to face with Sal Zaldivar.

"What's going on Sal?"

"On my way to hear a great new band. *Liar.*"

"Where are they playing?"

"Right here." Sal grabbed Holly's arm and pulled her towards the Last Day Saloon. "I need a volunteer to sit with me, enjoy the music, and not talk options or programming for the rest of the night."

"I am your gal," laughed Holly as they headed into Last Day.

Maybe Friday wouldn't turn out to be so horrible after all.

DUE DILIGENCE

$

Sunday * December 5, 1999
6:19 PM

"What are we going to do? They uncovered patent infringement."

"Due diligence uncovered some technology patent problems," said Tom Samoley as he sipped his Glenlevich and smiled at Milena. He adjusted the chair in the corner of the splurch.com executive loft to full lay out and turned the vibrator to high.

"If we don't own that patent to our technology we don't have a company," said Milena. She stood at the loft rail and watched four splurch.com employees play a raucous game of Foosball below her.

"A minor problem."

"Minor problem," repeated Milena. The players finished their game and poured out the front door. Her dreams of financial independence slowly began to disappear into a sea of lawyer insanity.

"We filed a patent, right?"

"Of course, but it hasn't been approved yet, and somehow that inventor bozo had his patent approved, so ours probably won't."

"You worry too much. The patent office is clueless. They rubber stamp all new web patents." said Tom as he finished his drink. "No matter what."

"Hey Milena – I am taking off now." A voice jolted Milena out of her nightmare. Sal Zaldivar was crossing the front office below her with his bike on his shoulder.

"I didn't know you came in today," said Milena.

"Somebody has to keep the site cooking," said Sal. ""The web doesn't take Sunday off. It's a 24-7 kind of thing."

17

"The internet has no religion," laughed Tom.

"You be careful Sal," admonished Milena in her most motherly tone. "It's almost Christmas. There are going to be tons of holiday shoppers on the road, and it's already dark."

"I'll be careful." Sal said as he smiled up at her. "I've been riding my bike in this city for three years and I've never had an accident."

"Is there a light on that bike?"

"Yes, Mom," said Sal. "and one attached to my leg, and one on my arm, and – oh look – there's a large reflector on the back of the seat."

"That's good."

"I am wearing bright clothing and a hat that is covered with reflective tape," continued Sal as he spun around and modeled his night biking attire. "Now do I have my CEO's permission to bike on the San Francisco streets of danger?"

"We don't want you to get hurt Sal," said Milena. "We need everyone healthy and pushing the splurch.com apple cart."

"Splurch rules," laughed Sal as he opened the door and pushed his bike out into a street teaming with dot com nightlife.

"You're good," said Tom from his vibrating throne. "Milena Peterson is a Chief Executive Officer that knows how to relate to her employees."

"I am the best," said Milena as she turned to face him. "That's why you hired me."

"The investors all agreed. You were our first choice."

"If we don't get the IPO done, I am in trouble. There will be no pot of gold at the end of the rainbow because there will be no rainbow. And my resume is going to look pretty bleak if every other CEO in California takes their company public and I can't figure out how to do it."

"Milena don't worry," said Tom as he sipped his drink.

"Easy for you to say, Mr. Silverspoon in your mouth since day one," sighed Milena. "The investment banking firm says they might drop us because of the patent problem. If they do that, all the stock you venture guys set aside for me would be worth somewhere between twelve cents and nothing."

Tom climbed out of the vibrating chair and walked to Milena.

"We WILL get the splurch.com IPO done," said Tom. "I guarantee it."

"If they drop us, who will do it?"

"We'll find somebody," said Tom. "There are an awful lot of greedy companies out there who want to get their hands on some of those big IPO bucks."

"What about the patent infringement?" asked Milena.

"When we get our patent, we'll counter sue, and settle out of court for an exchange of rights. No sweat."

"No sweat," repeated Milena.

"And we can always purchase patent infringement insurance," continued Tom.

"They sell insurance for patent infringement?" asked Milena.

"They sell insurance for everything."

The splurch.com front door flew open. A bearded man in a stained Santa suit came stumbling through the door waving a bottle of tequila. He weaved across the floor, flopped onto the the Foosball table, and smiled up at Milena and Tom.

"Happy Holidays."

OFF SITE

Monday * December 6, 1999
5:09 AM

It had to be a mistake, thought Norm. My name isn't on the new organizational chart because of a simple mistake. Splurch.com needs engineers like me – no matter how old and decrepit.

It's a mistake.

Norm was driving into San Francisco two hours early. He'd be the first Monday morning arrival. He'd show everybody how dedicated to the cause old Norm was.

Norm cruised north on 280 through the early morning dark and fog. He thought about the rest of the week after he heard that he wasn't on the new organizational chart. He tried to be good and not antagonize Milena, but it seemed honesty was exactly the wrong policy when it came to working with her.

When Milena had asked what he thought about the new logo, he had tried to be diplomatic.

He had cleared his cache and started loading the splurch.com home page. He pointed at the bottom of the screen where the percentage of the page that was downloaded was being displayed. After three seconds it was still less than ten percent. "It's too big," he said.

"It's not too big... it only takes up a quarter of the page. And it looks great," snapped Milena as she leaned in and watched the splurch.com logo slowly unfold on Norm's screen.

"I don't mean too big on the page. I mean the file is too large," said Norm. He leaned away from the screen and glanced up at Milena's face hovering only inches from his screen. Milena's best friend, Addy Lister, had created the new logo. Addy lived in a loft space across the Bay Bridge in Emeryville. She built a splurch.com sculpture out of mud, leaves, and CD disks. She photographed the sculpture, and scanned it into Photoshop. Milena and Addy had spent a month working on the design until they were sure the final image encapsulated "everything" that was splurch.com.

"You are not fucking up this logo," said Milena as she turned and looked down at Norm. Her lips were set in the firm corporate line she used when she was unwilling to listen to any arguments from her underlings. "Sal showed me what it would look like if we cut the file size down. It looked horrible. Really awful. It's important that people know immediately when they arrive at splurch.com what they're in for. This logo visually tells them. It works."

"But it takes too long to download. People aren't going to hang around to find out what splurch.com is because they are going to give up and click to another site. You know that the average web surfer waits less than ten seconds for a site to download," said Norm in the most non-combative voice he could muster.

"I guess splurch.com will have to appeal to the non-average web surfer," said Milena as she put her finger on Norm's computer screen and tapped on the new logo.

Norm hated it when people touched his screen. Just hated it. Milena did it all the time. He wanted to tell her to stop but every time they were in the middle of an argument about something or other and it never seemed appropriate. Maybe she did it in the middle of their arguments just to piss him off. Maybe he would put an anonymous post-it-note on her computer screen describing the horrible things that happened to people who touched other people's computer screens.

When Norm got to splurch.com, he found a parking place on Harrison. A remarkable achievement that must have had something to do with it being 5:30 AM.

Norm walked into the office, made coffee, and started working. First man on the job. Good job Norm!

At seven, Norm looked around. No one else had arrived. Strange.

At eight, he looked around again. Still just him. Weird.

By nine, Norm was panicked. Where was everyone?

At nine thirty one of the new tatooed employees walked in the door.

"Where is everybody?" asked Norm.

"They're having an off site meeting today, Milena asked me to handle the phones "til the meeting was over."

"About what?" asked Norm trying to stem the fear in his voice.

"The Christmas party and building security."

"Off site meeting," whispered Norm as he stared at his computer screen. "An off-site meeting that everyone is invited to but me."

December 6, 1999

Schools Scramble for Internet Degrees

EXPLORATORIUM

Monday * December 6, 1999
8:11 PM

"You are?" asked the blonde haired woman.

"Holly Chen."

The blonde scanned the table covered with name tags in the lobby of the Exploratorium.

"With?"

"Splurch.com." replied Holly.

"Never heard of Splurch.com," said the woman looking past Holly at the line growing behind her.

"You will soon," smiled Holly, "we're doing billboards next month."

"Splurch.com isn't on our master list," she said glancing down at the list on her clipboard.

Oh great, thought Holly as the Gate Keeper did another impatient search through the name tags. This is how I want to spend my Monday night. Trying to get into a party that I don't want to attend in the first place.

"Do you know when your company returned the RSVP?"

"I don't think we got an official invitation," said Holly.

"That would explain it," Blondie said immediately.

Holly's apartment mates had promised to join her at the party for the free food and drink, but, at the last minute, all claimed they were too tired and were now on the couch in their pj's waiting for "Ally McBeal." Holly figured she could get home and be on the couch with them in less than twenty minutes.

splurch.com

"Someone called my CEO, Milena Peterson, and invited splurch.com," explained Holly. "I am here because she promised someone would show up."

"Sorry," said Blondie, "I can only let people into the party who have official invitations."

"Fine," said Holly. "I'll tell my CEO you wouldn't let me in."

Holly turned and collided with a man in an expensive leather jacket.

"Sorry," Holly gasped.

"No problem," said the smiling man. "We're not going to let this beautiful young woman escape our party are we Diane?"

"She's not on the list, Phil."

"What company are you with?"

"Splurch.com," said Holly. "But you have a whole line of people waiting to get into this party and you won't miss one administrative assistant."

"Splurch.com... is it a John Samoley company?"

"John is Tom Samoley's father. Tom is our principal investor."

"Then you are my personal guest," said Phil picking up a pen and a blank name tag. "What's your name?"

"Holly Chen."

"You're an administrative assistant at Splurch.com?"

"Officially, I am an associate producer but I do whatever the CEO tells me, so administrative assistant is more accurate."

"Like coming to this party?" joked Phil as he pinned the hand-made name tag on Holly's jacket.

"That's right," said Holly as they headed into the Exploratorium.

Holly and Phil climbed the stairs to the upper level where the food and liquor were flowing and the music was ear-shatteringly loud. The Krevix IPO had hit the street that morning, and the stock price had skyrocketed. If the price stayed up until the end of the 180 day lockout period, most of these party-goers were going to be very wealthy and the fact that it was a Monday night wasn't slowing anybody's celebration.

"I should concentrate on schmoozing major players," Holly shouted as they wormed their way through the packed party. "If you point out a major player or two I would appreciate it"

"Standing in front of the sound wave exhibit is Mitawoksi Galandhi. He's the genius who invented the technology for this company," shouted Phil.

"Great."

"Next to the echo chamber is Eleanor Farthner and James Smiley, two of the Board members. Playing with the kids in the shadow box is Grace Smerdon. She's from Visa. They are one of the Krevix's strategic partners."

"Perfect," said Holly. "That's enough to get me started."

"You could schmooze me a little," laughed Phil.

"You're the official party problem solver," declared Holly. "Right?"

"Close," said Phil.

"Need you backstage, Phil," a man yelled from across the room.

Phil glanced at his watch. "On my way."

"I have to do something and unfortunately when it's over I have to do some schmoozing of my own," said Phil as he smiled into Holly's eyes. "May I call you sometime and schedule a drink or something?"

"Sounds like fun," said Holly searching her pockets." I don't have a card but, if you give me your card, I'll e-mail you my number."

"Sounds like a plan," laughed Phil as he handed her his card. "It was great meeting you."

As Phil disappeared into the crowd, Holly looked at the expensive business card he had placed in her hand.

Holly flashed on the headline she had seen in the morning paper.

SKYROCKETING IPO MAKES STEINBERG 2 MILLION DOLLARS IN FIRST HOUR OF TRADING.

Holly had been flirting with a man who made 2 million dollars an hour.

Definitely worth missing Ally McBeal.

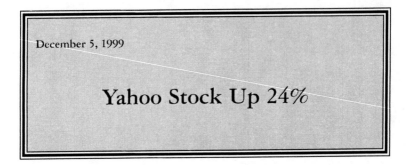

ULTIMATE FRISBEE

Wednesday * December 8, 1999
4:34 PM

Sal rose as high as he could but the disc sailed past his outstretched hand.

Damn!

If he had caught it, he could have scored.

Sal watched as the BUG ZAPPING CIRCUS defender picked up the gleaming green Frisbee and sent it flying back up the field with a perfect snap of the wrist.

"If you had grabbed that huck we would have scored," sang Beth from the other side of the field.

"I know Beth," yelled Sal as they both watched the BUG ZAPPING CIRCUS team whip the Frisbee closer and closer towards the goal at the other end of the field.

"Too short," laughed Beth as they started trotting up the field, "two inches taller and you'd have grabbed the pass and this game would be over."

"Ha ha ha," hollered Sal, "I'd have scored if you hadn't thrown it seven miles over my head."

"That was a perfect huck," said Beth as they watched the action at the other end of the field. "Any lower and that guy would have intercepted."

"You could have thrown around him," said Sal.

"Give it up Sal," laughed Beth. "Climb out of the darkness and see the light. You have a shortness problem. You just need to grow a little."

Sal Zaldivar had been playing on the BETTER LIVING THROUGH INSANITY co-ed ultimate Frisbee team for four years. He was the best player on the team and was seriously considering joining an all

27

male team and find out how good he really was. But, he was five feet three inches. That was pretty dang short.

Suddenly, an INSANITY defender intercepted a slightly errant BUG huck. The Frisbee was coming back towards them. Sal sprinted up field to put some distance between himself and the BUG defender.

"I'll be there," screamed Beth as she headed up field.

The green Frisbee was now flying towards Sal through the patches of fog that slowly drifted across the Beach Chalet playing fields.

Sal laid out and grabbed the disc just before it hit the ground. He spun and fired to Beth who was charging towards their goal with a defender frantically trying to keep up.

The pass was perfect. Beth caught the spinning green disc and scored with ease. Game over.

Sal was unlocking his bike in the parking lot after the game, when Beth wrapped her arms around from behind.

"Just kidding Sal," Beth whispered in his ear, "you're just the right size for me."

"You wish," said Sal as he climbed aboard his bike. "Beat ya to the Chalet."

"I doubt that," said Beth as she leaped into a convertible full of INSANIACS that screeched to a stop behind her.

Sal raced his bike out of the lot and thought about his shortness. He was thirty-one years old and done growing. Somebody told him that once you stopped growing you started shrinking. He'd never get any taller. He actually might get shorter. Not a pleasant thought.

"You're gonna lose this race," Sal yelled over his shoulder at the INSANIAC convertible as they raced down JFK Drive towards the Great Highway that divided Golden Gate Park from Ocean Beach.

Maybe his shortness was some kind of divine balancing act. He had always been the smartest guy at school and now was Milena's "gun slinger." He could solve Splurch.com's computer problems faster and more elegantly than anybody else.

Work had been difficult today. All Norm talked about was not being invited to the Monday off site meeting even though it was only because his name had been mistakenly left off the list. Holly spent the entire day talking about the dot com millionaire she had met at a party and asking for Sal's help in wording the e-mail she was sending him.

"Give up that gas guzzler," shouted Sal as he pulled into the Beach Chalet Brewery inches in front of the convertible.

Sal had a great time with Holly at the Last Day Saloon. He had thought about asking her back to his place, but he was on the bike and it seemed too awkward. Besides, Holly was nine years younger than he was, she was Asian and he was Salvadoran, she was cute and he was ugly, they were co-workers, and....

Sure, thought Sal as he climbed the stairs past the Depression era murals on the Beach Chalet walls. I didn't ask Holly back to my place because I'm chicken, and now she's going to be dating a dot com millionaire.

Way to go, Sal.

December 9, 1999

IPO Fever Hotter Than Ever

ENERGIZED

Friday * December 10, 1999
5:22 PM

"Imagine that the iron circle surrounding your body is slowly sinking into the earth," intoned Alexis. "Deeper and deeper it sinks."

Milena tried to focus on the energy healer's words.

"You are approaching the molten core. The lava is glowing."

This was Milena's third session with her energy healer. The first sessions had been overwhelmingly enjoyable and productive. For the past few weeks she had felt calmer than she had in months.

"Your iron energy shield is making contact with the glowing lava," said Alexis from her rocking chair in the pleasantly decorated basement room that served as the healing center in her Sunset home. "Your iron circle is beginning to sink into the boiling lava. You are about to connect to the earth's core."

Milena tried to think about connecting to the earth's core, and not about the splurch.com problems that were racing through her brain just like they did when they woke her up every morning at 4:30 AM.

"Feel the power of the earth flowing into your body. Feel your tensions flowing out," chanted Alexis.

Milena felt the tension start to leave her body. It was working again. Thank God.

"Have you made contact with the earth's core yet?" asked Alexis.

"I think so," said Milena as she stretched out on the futon across the room from Alexis.

"Can you feel the tension leaving your body?"

"Yes," whispered Milena. "But it doesn't feel like a totally free flow."

"That's right Milena. There's a block in your flow. A very large block."

"What is it?" asked Milena "What do you think is blocking me."

"I see a man holding a large amount of money in his hands," said Alexis after a brief pause.

"That would be Tom Samoley," said Milena immediately. "That guy is always making my life difficult."

"Why is that?" asked Alexis.

"Because he only thinks about what's best for Tom Samoley."

"He only thinks about himself?" asked Alexis.

"He also thinks about money. I don't know which one he thinks about more. It would be a close race," laughed Milena.

"Why don't you remove this man from your life?" questioned Alexis.

"You don't remove the lead investor from your life," sighed Milena. "Especially when you're the CEO of his company."

"I am seeing a past life relationship with Tom Samoley," said Alexis.

"That sounds right," said Milena, "Tom has been making my life miserable forever."

"It's possible that you have been working on this relationship for more than a couple of lifetimes," said Alexis.

As Alexis began an exploration of Milena's past life struggles with Tom Samoley, Milena felt herself relax. She was continually surprised to discover how much this "different" kind of therapy helped.

For the final half hour of the session, Alexis focused on specific exercises Milena could use to deal with the insecurities of the "on again-off again" splurch.com IPO. Alexis also talked about Milena's thirty eight year old biological clock and why she never seemed to be able to find the man she was looking for.

Milena knew exactly why she couldn't find the perfect guy. He didn't exist.

After the session, Milena sat in her Mercedes and watched the sun sink through flaming red clouds into the Pacific Ocean.

San Francisco was such a beautiful place to live.

Milena pulled the cell phone out of her Gucci bag. She smiled as she turned it on and thought about her first energy healing session when she had forgotten to turn it off. It rang just as she was reaching the earth's core, and Milena was firmly informed that a cell phone would never again be part of one of Alexis's healing sessions.

The phone started chirping immediately.

"This is Milena."

"Milena, this is Holly."

"Holly, I told you not to call me on my cell after work unless it was extremely important," Milena explained patiently.

"This is extremely important."

"What?"

"You have to go to San Francisco General Emergency Room," Holly started sobbing. "I don't know if he has insurance so maybe they won't admit him, or they won't treat him, or they won't..."

"Who" shouted Milena as tension shot through her entire body.

"Sal. A stupid Muni driver hit him while he was riding his bike on Market Street."

"Oh my God."

DOYLE DRIVE

$

Monday * December 13, 1999
11:03 AM

Tom handed the friendly Golden Gate Bridge toll collector three crisp dollar bills and thought about the meeting he had just left. He had won. Again.

Nobody would ever know that Tom Samoley – with the perfect Sand Hill Road business address – now owned a pornographic web site. He reached into his breast pocket, pulled out his cell phone, and hit his Dad's speed dial.

After one ring, a Southern drawl exploded from the miniature speaker, "Better be pretty damn important because I am about to birdie this hole and win another thousand dollars from these suckers."

"We did it Dad."

"They went for it?"

"Like bears to honey."

"How much MORE did you offer 'em," barked John Samoley.

"Offered 'em LESS," laughed Tom. "They were just too excited about selling to legitimate businessmen."

"Did you tell them that your Dad made his millions in the home video business," chortled John. "That renting porno made me the man I am today."

"Didn't bring it up."

"Great job. Now let me go back to extracting money from these amateurs. They were talking smack until they realized it's impossible to beat a Samoley when there's money on the line."

"Ya got that right," smiled Tom as a sea of red tail lights suddenly started flashing in front of him. "Where are you playing today?"

"Olympic."

"I thought the Olympic didn't have tee times available," said Tom squeezing the brakes of his Ferrari 360 Modena and stopping behind a line of cars waiting impatiently before the final dip in Doyle Drive.

"Until I told them the name of the fellow who wanted to play. Then they said no problem. No problem at all. OUT."

The phone clicked in Tom's ear. John Samoley was tuning into the Jim Rome show every morning and had been adding some of Rome's verbal pyrotechnics to his own explosive delivery.

Purchasing a porno web site was the perfect move, thought Tom as he peered over the line of stopped cars in front of him. Not only were porn sites pulling in wads of cash, they had best technology out there. Porn sites worked. The digital pictures and graphics were optimized for instant download. The streaming videos were state of the art. Their servers didn't crash and their e-commerce solutions were the best. Maybe if he got some of those porno web tech whizzes working for him, he'd figure out how to make real money with the under-achieving internet start ups he and his Dad invested in.

Tom turned on KGO. The all-news station had traffic and weather every ten minutes. The Samoley luck held. The traffic report was just starting.

"In San Francisco, there's injury accident working in front of the Exploratorium in the Marina," explained the KGO announcer, "avoid the Doyle Drive exit."

Tom hit the speed dial for Milena's cell phone.

She picked up half way through the first ring.

"I'm stuck," drawled Tom.

"I'm Milena. Glad you called Stuck," joked Milena.

"A CEO with a sense of humor. How unusual," laughed Tom. "What's happening at my favorite dot com."

"You say that to all your dot coms."

"Yes I do."

"Sal Zaldivar got hit by a bus."

"Our boy genius?"

"Yes."

"How many hours did it take for splurch.com to crash?"

"You have no faith. I have it under control. Norm Dotoshay is picking up the slack."

"The opinionated old hacker."

"That's right."

"You have your work cut out for you Milena."

"Yes I do."

CLICK

The KGO announcer began describing another bullish day on Wall Street. What a sexy voice, thought Tom. If she looks half as good as she sounds, she's my kind of woman.

Tom glanced at the narrow band of roadway between the line of cars and the freeway wall. It wasn't that far back to the Lombard Exit. He slowly turned his car around and headed back towards the exit. The blare of the horns from the line of cars he was squeezing past was deafening.

Tom hit his office speed dial.

"Samoley Ventures," a pleasant voice vibrated in his ear.

"Judy, can you get me the number of the Station Manager of KGO. It's in the Rolodex. I met him at fund raiser a couple of months ago."

"Sure thing Tom."

"I am going to call and see if I can take him and one of his announcers to lunch," said Tom as he slipped past the last blaring horn and accelerated down the exit ramp.

God he loved this life.

SF GENERAL

Tuesday * December 14, 1999
2:27 PM

Stupid stupid stupid.

Sal looked at the casts on his arm and leg and said it one more time.

Stupid.

How long had he been riding a bike in San Francisco? Three years? There was no excuse for his stupidity.

The Muni driver had signaled and Sal hadn't seen it. He had been looking at the dot com advertisement that was splashed across the entire bus. The bus blinker was covered with mud, but he still should have seen the signal and he didn't.

This was Day Four of sitting in a bed at San Francisco General Hospital with absolutely nothing to do but watch teenage girls on Sally Jessie Raphael explain how they cheated on their boyfriends.

Stupid.

Sal Zaldivar graduated from Stanford with a degree in engineering and had a job at splurch.com making eighty-five K a year. He was a graphic interface designer. He was an accomplished artist, a top of the line programmer, and an all round computer problem solving genius. He was a hot Bay Area commodity.

But, his trusty right hand was now non-functional. He was now just a blob of non-productive flesh sitting in a hospital bed watching a commercial about how to defend yourself from "your worst sweat."

Stupid.

The phone rang. Sal reached over with his left hand and awkwardly brought the receiver to his ear.

"Sal Zaldivar."

"Hi Sal," the pleasant sounding woman on the other end of the line replied. "This is Kelly Render with the Premiere Insurance Group."

"Is this is about my accident?"

"Yes. We were contacted by splurch.com, but we don't have your name on the official list of splurch.com employees."

"I've been working there for over a year."

"But we can't start processing your claim until we have confirmation that you're actually employed by splurch.com."

"Just call em," Sal said. "Everybody knows I work there."

"We need official documentation," said Kelly.

"So how do you get that?" asked Sal.

"I'll mail the form to splurch.com today," said Kelly. "just make sure that somebody official returns it to Premiere as soon as possible."

"Great. I'll call Holly and tell her to watch for it," said Sal.

"I'll make sure the form gets in the mail this week," said Kelly cheerily. "Have a wonderful day."

"You too," grumbled Sal as she clicked off.

I sure hope this isn't going to be a problem he thought as he watched a tattooed bleached blonde on the television explain to her repentant dread-lock boyfriend what true love means.

Health insurance was always screwed up. Last month, one of the splurch.com designers had developed repetitive stress syndrome and Milena had offered him a lump sum payment if he quit. She said it was because his therapy was taking too much work time but Sal wondered if she had gotten pressure from the insurance company to just dump him.

The phone rang again.

Sal answered and the receiver exploded in his ear.

"Zaldivarrrrrrrrrr"

"Hey Mart."

Martino Dekench was Sal's Stanford freshman roomate "When are you coming down to interview?" Mart shouted.

"Totally out of commission right now."

"Nobody cares. They just want you. Arrive for the interview with third degree burns over 95% of your body and you'll still get a job offer."

"What an unpleasant thought," said Sal.

"Working with me?" joked Mart.

"That too," laughed Sal.

"You know what kind of bonus the last guy they hired got?".

"Thirty thousand dollars?"

"A BMW Z-3 roadster with 2.8 liter V-6."

"I ride a bike," responded Sal.

"He has 24-7 use of the car as long as he works here. They even let him gas at the company pump for free."

"What about starting our own company?" asked Sal, "Isn't that what we decided to do to make some real bucks?"

"Got an idea yet?"

"I am working on it."

A serious, well-dressed woman walked into Sal's hospital room.

"Got a visitor," said Sal. "Gotta go."

"Salvidor Zaldivar?" the woman asked from the foot of his bed.

"That's me," said Sal.

"We have a problem," said the woman as the lines in her face deepened.

"Problem?"

"Premiere says they no longer insure splurch.com."

KINKO'S

Wednesday * December 15, 1999
3:39 PM

"MAC or PC floppy?"

Holly stood in front of the Kinko's computer desk shaking her head. "I have no idea. We use both. I should have asked somebody before I left."

"No problem. I'll check it for you," said the blue shirted Kinko's employee. "Either way it could be awhile. There's about a thirty minute wait for the PC's and forty-five for the MACs."

It turned out to be a MAC disk and the wait was over an hour.

Holly watched the Kinko's human ebb and flow. Her Kinko's buddy had quit over the weekend, so now she was going to have to figure out how to get this promotional page printed and copied out all by her lonesome. Major pain in the butt.

Dot commers of all ages were racing around trying to get the machines to do their bidding and meet another drop dead deadline. Holly was certain the machines could sense their user's frantic need and were automatically shutting down whenever a certain level of insanity was reached.

Sitting and thinking was not what Holly needed to be doing right now. She had finally sent Phil Steinberg an e-mail with her phone numbers that was absolutely perfect – funny, witty, and short.

So far, no response. Damn.

Finally, Holly was able to sit down at one of the MACs. She figured out how to use Adobe Illustrator to open the files but none of the pictures embedded in the page would appear on the screen. Hoping the photos were just not showing up on the monitor, Holly printed the file. The printer spit out the image immediately – but there were blank white spaces where the pictures were supposed to be.

splurch.com

What to do now?

Holly had a flash. She would call Sal at the hospital. He had worked on the file before his bike accident and he now wasn't doing anything but watching television.

There was a courtesy phone at Kinko's somewhere. Holly spent ten minutes trying to capture the attention of an over-gothic looking Kinko's employee to find out where it was, but finally decided to try to find a pay phone.

"I'll be right back," Holly chirped at the line of people staring at her machine as she flew out the front door. "Really. This will only take a minute."

The market next door to Kinko's had a pay phone but there were two Latino girls chatting on it.

Holly stood as close to the phone as possible. She smiled broadly at the giggling teenagers every time they looked in her direction, and prayed that one of the people waiting at Kinko's didn't decide to hijack her Mac while she wasn't there to protect her turf.

"Holly, why didn't you open the "Read Me" file that was on that disk?" Sal asked as soon as he got on the phone. "I told Milena. It explains everything."

"She didn't tell me to do that."

"That's Milena."

"Can ya give me a simple quick way to getting those pretty pictures on the screen?"

"When the file opened did a dialogue box appear?"

"Yep. I hit continue like I always do."

"That box is asking you where the pictures are. When it appears you need to go to the submaster folder and open the presentation picture file," explained Sal.

"Of course," laughed Holly. "How could I not know that."

Holly raced back to the Kinko's, found the pictures, placed them in the document, and printed the page out - on the wrong size paper.

40

Holly tried three times to print the file but each time it ended up on the wrong size paper. A Kinko's employee eventually arrived and got the correct size page printed, but vertically instead of horizontally. They adjusted the page set up and finally got a perfect print.

The wait for the color copier was over an hour and three times Holly had to find another Kinko's savior to soothe the machine back into operation to get her hundred copies made.

It took thirty more minutes for Holly to pay the bill and start back to splurch.com.

"Two hundred forty three dollars and seventeen cents?" Milena asked as she stared at the receipt Holly handed her. "It took you an hour of computer time to print out one page?"

Holly stared at the receipt. "Sorry Milena, I am not real focused today."

"Holly, you have to pay more attention to your job."

"I agree."

"Maybe you'll be more focused after you return the phone call you just got."

"Phone call?"

"From a Phil Steinberg."

"Yesssssssss."

E-MAIL

Friday * December 17, 1999
7:31 AM

From: Justine Peterson [mail to:justineP@earthlink.net]
Sent: Thursday, December 17, 1999 6:17 am
To: Milena_Peterson@splurch.com
Subject: Holidays

Milena:

Have you decided when you are flying to Florida yet? The Ramunsons are planning a pool dinner party on the night of Thursday the 23rd and are really hoping you'll make it.

I finally watched Ally McBeal like you suggested. It's too crazy for me.

Let me know your plans, asap.

Love, Mom

From: Tom Samoley [mail to:Tom@SamoleyVentures.com]
Sent: Thursday, December 17, 1999 6:34 am
To: Milena_Peterson@splurch.com
Subject: Re: Galinzo Group

can't make 4...you'll have to work it out with them yourself...

t

Milena wrote:

>The meeting is scheduled at 4 pm here. It will be difficult. They
>think we have a done deal & will not be happy about any changes.

>Milena Peterson
>Chief Executive Officer
>Splurch.com

Tom Samoley wrote:

>>Let me know the meeting time and place. I have looked over the contract

>>and I think we should reduce their percentage by 2%

> > What do you think?

> >t

From: Adrianna Lister [mail to:artaddy@hotmail.com]
Sent: Thursday, December 17, 1999 6:42 am
To: Milena_Peterson@splurch.com
Subject: Come to Weekend Fun!!!!!!!!!!

hey mil...

just bugging you one more time... ya got to come up and meet us at Tahoe this weekend. You have to come. Screw that job. You have to come. This is an order from your best friend.

I am taking off in the next hour or so and will be there up through tuesday but it doesn't matter when you come... just come... you could come up late Saturday night and leave early sunday morn and everybody would just be happy to see ya.

Screw splurch!!!!

time off will help.. really...you'll make more accurate corporate decisions... your karma will increase and draw more positive stuff your way... come.... it's the holidaze.... it's going to be fun... Chuck and Sandy are buying a pig that we are going to barbecue on Saturday (or whatever you do with pigs) and i am going to hide some cooked pig and a bottle of scotch in a secret Milena place and when you get here Saturday night we'll have a party together.

Come up to Tahoe.... come up to fun...

Screw splurch.

your pal, Addy

Get Your Private, Free Email at http://www.hotmail.com

From: Selenor Galinzo [mail to:Selenor_Galinzo@GalinzoGroup.com]
Sent: Thursday, December 17, 1999 7:01am
To: Milena_Peterson@splurch.com
Subject: Today's Meeting

Milena:

Confirming that we will be at Splurch at 4 PM today.

I am bringing champagne, Kathy is bringing cookies, and we are both looking

43

splurch.com

forward to a long and profitable relationship between the Galinzo Group and splurch.com

Best Regards,

Selenor

From: Justine Peterson [mail to:justineP@earthlink.net]
Sent: Thursday, December 17, 1999 7:03 am
To: Milena_Peterson@splurch.com
Subject: More Holidays

I forgot to ask you if you bought that golf bag for your father. I think it's a good idea because I hear through the grapevine that he has been playing on that course near Disney World every other day.

I invited him to join us for Christmas dinner but have not heard back & of course I don't really expect to.

More Love, Mom

Date: 12/16 9:02 pm
Received: 12/17 7:10 am
From: be_a_trader@boohoo.com
Reply-To: currency@orderspec.com
To: www@www.www

Free video http://www.orderspec.com/commodity/

FREE VIDEO ABOUT STOCKS AND COMMODITIES

Learn how to make money in the commodity markets by using options.
Learn how to use leverage to your advantage.
Learn how to use risk control money management.
Learn the secrets of how to forecast markets.

LEARN HOW TO PROTECT PROFITS

LEARN HOW TO MAKE MONEY IN A DOWN MARKET.

LEARN HOW TO CHANGE YOUR LIFE.

LEARN HOW TOFREE YOURSELF FROM FINANCIAL WORRY

LEARN HOW TO GUARANTEE YOUR FUTURE

For removal from future mailings, click on reply and type REMOVE ME in the subject line.

Thanks!

From: Christine Baldwin [mail to:CBaldwin@jeeperz.com]
Sent: Thursday, December 17, 1999 7:15 am
To: Milena_Peterson@splurch.com
Subject: Saturday Conference

Milena:

This is to confirm that you and Tom Samoley will be attending the Jeeperz Awards this Saturday December 18 at 6 pm at the North Beach Restaurant.

If you are unable to attend please let us know.

Christine Baldwin
Co-ordinating ProducerJeeperz Awards

From: Holly Chen [mail to: Holly_Chen@splurch.com
Sent: Monday, December 17, 1999 7:27 am
To: Milena_Peterson@splurch.com
Subject: Breakfast Date

Milena:

Just a reminder that I'll be in a little late this morning cause I am meeting Phil Steinberg for breakfast.

Wish me luck.

Holly

December 17, 1999

Adobe Income Soars 94%

CLIFF HOUSE

Friday * December 17, 1999
9:56 AM

"Eleven?"

"I wanted to be a rock guitar player."

"Twelve?"

"A professional baseball player. Shortstop."

"Thirteen?"

"At thirteen I had my bar mitzvah. The day after the party, my Dad took me into his office, dramatically closed the door, and handed me a key to the office safe. "Welcome to the business Phil.""

"That's when you decided that you wanted to be a business man?" asked Holly.

"No," laughed Phil. "That's when I decided I wanted to be ANY-THING BUT A BUSINESSMAN."

"But you're a businessman now."

"I am an entrepreneur. I don't make widgets. I create companies that make widgets," said Phil.

"What's the difference?"

Phil stared out the window and watched the waves crash onto Seal Rock. Holly had arrived Upstairs at the Cliff House with Phil at 8 AM. When they sat down for omelets at 8:10, they'd agreed to race out the door by 9. It was now 9:57.

"I think the difference is huge but it probably exists only in my mind," Phil said. "Your turn. What did you want to be when you were ten years old?"

"A ballerina," said Holly, "but I might have wanted to be a cowboy by then."

"Cowboy?"

"I had this book called THE BIG BOOK OF HORSES. There was a picture of a cowboy riding this dappled grey stallion and twirling a rope over his head. The caption said something about about how the cowboy and the horse were such great partners. Right then I decided I wanted to be a cowboy."

"So what did you want to be when you were eleven?"

"A cowboy."

"Twelve?"

"I was now searching for the perfect horse. My bedroom walls were covered with pictures of every kind of horse I could find."

"Not a cowgirl?"

"I didn't know if cowgirls were allowed to be partners with horses," laughed Holly.

"Did you still want to be a cowboy when you were thirteen?"

"I kissed Kevin Wong at my thirteenth birthday party and didn't want to be partners with horses any more."

"What did you want to be?"

"In love."

Phil's coffee cup momentarily froze and Holly's mind exploded in a silent scream. Why did she say that? What a stupid thing to say? She had crossed the line. She was doing so well and now ahhhhhhhh.

"Is that what you want now?" Phil said quietly. "To be in love?"

Holly smiled and took a sip of coffee. She needed time to come up with a witty response.

"Isn't that what we all want?" she finally said.

"Perfect response," laughed Phil, "love is what all humans are looking for."

They both smiled, and sipped their coffee. Holly breathed a mental sigh of relief. Great response Holly. Way to go. You have this relationship business down!

Phil glanced at his watch and immediately pulled out his cell phone. "Do you mind if I make a quick call? I should let everyone know I am going to be late for today's dog and pony show."

"No problem," said Holly as she bounced out of her chair. "It's time I made a journey downstairs anyway."

"Great," said Phil as he punched numbers into his cell phone.

Holly walked down the stairs past a series of old black and white photos. People in full body swimming suits were cavorting in a large indoor swimming pool filled with Pacific Ocean water. A hundred years ago, Land's End was the center of San Francisco recreational universe.

Holly stopped at the pay phone on her way out of the women's rest room and called Milena.

"Milena, I am going to be later than I thought."

"There's something I need to know," said Milena seriously.

"Did I screw up again?"

"I need to know how the omelet date is going with the boy millionaire?"

Holly breathed a sigh of relief. "Great," she whispered.

"Wait," Milena said. "I am putting you on the speaker phone."

"Noooooo," laughed Holly. "Don't do that."

Phil suddenly appeared at the top of the stairs carrying Holly's jacket. "We have to roll," he shouted. "Crisis at headquarters."

Phil and Holly walked out the Cliff House front door and were immediately swimming through a river of tourists being disgorged from two large red buses. When they cleared the crowd, Phil turned to Holly and said, "I am flying to Bangalore, India tomorrow morning. Want to go?"

Decision time.

HOSPITAL CHRISTMAS

Saturday * December 18, 1999
5:23 AM

Sal heard the Christmas carols echoing through the SF General corridors for over an hour before the first smiling caroler burst into his room, straightened his top hat, and started *om-pa-pa-ing* at the foot of his bed.

Three of his old time English caroler pals poured into the room and began a four part rendition of "God Rest Ye Merry Gentlemen."

Sal groaned on the inside but smiled on the outside.

The Quartet finished with a flourish and immediately launched into a sprightly version of "Here comes Santa Claus" as a jolly Rent-A-Santa came ho-ho-hoing into the room.

"And what do you want for Christmas young man?" laughed the not very portly part-time Claus.

"To get out of the hospital," responded Sal.

"Santa can't do anything about that. Only Mother Nature can help you there."

"Got a way I can get in touch with her?"

"No, but I know someone who does," said Santa reaching into his bag of toys and pulling out a four color Jesus Saves brochure.

Sal stared at the picture of a weeping Christ on the cover. His inner groan exploded past his lips before he could get it under control.

"Don't underestimate the power of Jesus, son - especially at this time of year."

"Thanks," said Sal as he took the brochure with his uncasted left hand and placed it on the small pile of Christmas cards that were stacked on his night stand. "Could you try to get a hold of Him

49

tonight and see if He can send an army of angels to help break me out of this joint. And get Him to heal my cash appendage on the way out the door."

"Cash appendage?"

"My cash appendage," Sal said holding up the cast on his right arm. "This appendage codes faster than any appendage in Silicon Valley. This appendage can turn twenty lines of code into ten in a flash. This appendage draws original art that everyone loves. This appendage knows how to create the most intuitive graphics ever seen on the web. This is a big money appendage that is currently earning zip."

"Why don't you relax and enjoy the time off?" asked Santa as he sat on the edge of Sal's hospital bed.

"I wish I could," sighed Sal. "I guess my real problem is workaholism."

"Good luck," said Santa as he pulled a candy cane from his bag and placed it on the blanket covering Sal's chest." Santa has to go cheer up other patients now."

"There is something I really could use."

"What's that?"

"Health insurance."

"You work for a dot com. You have plenty of insurance."

"You would think so. But splurch.com was switching insurance companies at the time of my accident and now neither company wants to say, *Don't worry about it Sal. We'll pay the bill.*"

"It will get worked out."

"I hope so."

As the merry band of Christmas Cheerer-Upers left the room, Sal stared out the window at the fog covered Potrero Hill landscape. He was supposed to get out of the hospital on Tuesday but an anal retentive intern discovered potential spinal damage in his body x-ray, and they decided to keep him for two more days for tests and observation. Then on Thursday, the infection around the cuts on his broken arm spread to his lymph nodes. Surprise, surprise.

QUESTION: Where was the most likely place to get an infection?

ANSWER: A hospital.

Sal was leaving Sunday at noon and nobody was going to stop him. Even if his temperature shot to 104 degrees and gangrene covered his entire body - he was walking out that hospital front door.

The phone rang.

"Sal, glad I caught you in," laughed Norm.

"Not funny Norm."

"Sorry."

"So what's today's big web site trauma?"

"Well something is screwed up and I can't figure out what."

"What happened?"

"I was working on a new page, another one of Milena's insane ideas, and accidentally promoted the test site to the production site. Then we had a power outage and now I can't get anything to work "

"You at splurch now?"

"Yes."

"Okay. Let's take it step by step."

Sal talked to Norm for over an hour. It felt great to be working again - even if it was only in a half-ass consultant kind-of-way.

Sal wondered if he would get paid for helping Norm get the site back up. He wondered if splurch.com would actually talk one of their insurance companies into paying for his accident.

Embracing the unknown. What fun.

SOUTH PARK

Sunday * December 19, 1999
NOON

"Acorns."

"Acorns? Why are men like acorns?" laughed Holly as she stretched her toes toward the trees across from the South Park swing set that she and Milena were playing on.

Milena dropped her feet to the sand, and dragged herself to a stop. "What am I saying? Men aren't like acorns. Women are like acorns."

Holly stopped beside Milena. "Why are women like acorns?"

Milena smiled and said, "Oh no. I got it all wrong. Women aren't like acorns. Women are like avocados. Men are like bean sprouts." Milena leaned back, whipped her legs under her swing seat, and began pumping.

"You are making an alphabet joke." said Holly.

"Right. The twenty-sixth time you ask me what men are like I'll tell you that they're all zucchini," Milena said laughing and pumping herself higher and higher.

"And by the time men are like zucchini, what will women be like?"

"At the end of the alphabet there is no difference between men and women. Women are zucchini too."

"That makes no sense."

"There is your answer. Men and women make no sense."

Holly laughed and walked to the green metal bench at the edge of the sand filled playground as Milena continued to try to touch the sky with her toes.

It was Sunday noon but there was no appreciable slowdown in activity here in South Park, the epicenter of the dot com universe. For most dot commers Sunday was just a day to do extra maintenance on the dot com boilers.

Holly sat down on the bench and looked through the windows of the Ecco restaurant. Laughing patrons were enjoying their Sunday brunch. At the front counter a line of people waited for a noon jolt of joe to go. Christmas was only a week away, but it appeared that none of these web workers were taking time off to Christmas shop. Maybe if they worked hard enough, their dot com company would go public that much sooner and they would become dot com millionaires that much sooner, and then they would be able to take luxurious vacations and buy their loved ones expensive Christmas gifts.

Holly turned and watched a couple of ten year old boys race through the park on bikes with small wheels and big handle bars. They carried large plastic squirt guns and were spraying every person they passed. Most of their victims responded to the attack with good humor but a few shouts of anger followed the black adolescents as they pedaled out of the East end of the park laughing and screaming.

South Park was now the habitat of twenty-something Caucasian and Asian males, but, not that many years ago, it was a depressed area known as Heroin Alley. The transition had not been entirely smooth. Maybe, the squirt gun attack was an indication of how many of the former park residents felt about the dot com invaders.

Milena sat next to Holly on the bench.

"Are you going on the road with Phil the next time he asks? Or are you going to stay with me at splurch.com and help build the best business in the world?"

"I don't know," sighed Holly. "That's why I wanted to meet with you today. So you could help me figure it out."

"As your CEO, I vote you stay in San Francisco. As an older woman friend, I vote that you pack your bag and get on that next plane to wherever Phil asks you to go."

"But what if Phil turns out to be a jerk and I end up stuck in some foreign country with no way to get home?"

"Have him buy you a return ticket before you take off."

"What about Sal? I think he likes me. There might be something there down the road."

"As your CEO, I advise you to not get involved in office romances. As an older woman friend, I say Sal's a kind, generous, good looking fellow and that you should follow your animal instincts."

"We haven't slept together. Maybe our relationship is past that point already."

"Both the CEO and the older woman friend are out of advice."

"Milena you are no help."

"Did you really want advice?"

"Yes."

"Really?"

"Yes."

"The next time Phil asks - go with him."

"And you are saying that because I'll probably do the opposite of what you suggest."

"How did you guess?"

HIGHWAY 280

Monday * December 20, 1999
6:24AM

6:24 Dotoshay's lumpy green sofa. Norm clicks his home made universal remote through television channels and waits for his bagel to toast. He clicks through seven channels and hits the East Coast Sci-Fi Channel feed. A giant moth was attacking Tokyo. Norm had modified the dish in his backyard to pick up over 200 channels. He could get even more if he wanted to spend time hacking the satellite program. He didn't pay for anything - even the premium services. Just another benefit to being an old hacking fool, Norm thought as he watched a screaming moth attack the Japanese army.

6:42 280 North/85 split. So far so good. An accident on any of the highways criss-crossing San Jose turns the entire highway system into a parking lot. No accidents today. Should be clear sailing all the way to San Francisco.

6:45 De Anza/Apple Computer exit. This was Norm's exit for all the years he had been an Apple engineer. It was a secure job. He bought a house in San Jose. Then, Apple crumbled and Norm ended up out on the street with a lot of other smart people.

6:57 Sand Hill Road. Most of the VC firms that kept cash circulating in Silicon Valley were headquartered in one of the sprawling ranch style offices off this exit. Tom Samoley, the lead investor in splurch.com, has an office in one of the complexes. Norm was the third hire at splurch.com but had never set foot in Samoley Ventures. Maybe one of these mornings he should stop and ask 'em if they were interested in funding one of the ideas that Norm had percolating in his old hacker brain. Ha!

7:10 Highway 92. As his 95 Mazda passes two overturned RV's that had been pulled to the side of the road, Norm glances at the large sprawling lake on his left. What is that lake all about? Norm had been driving past the same lake for over twenty years and still didn't know it's name. Nobody is ever swimming or boating or doing anything in that lake. It looks man-made. One of these days he's going to ask somebody what the name of that lake is. Maybe it doesn't have a name. Nawww... All lakes have names. Even man-made lakes have names. Norm passes a sign that says that the stretch of highway has been adopted by AutoWeb. What an interesting thing to spend marketing dollars on. Sure hope AutoWeb is funded for the long haul. The long haul. Oh yeah.

7:31 Approaching 380. Decision time. Most mornings, Norm heads East on 380 towards the San Francisco airport, turns north onto 101, and then exits at Mission. If there is an accident anywhere on 101, he continues on 280 and takes the 6th Street exit.

7:32 KCBS. All news all the time. Detailed traffic reports every ten minutes. Everyone headed into San Francisco is checking KCBS as they approach this intersection. Whenever the station reports a problem, the lemming commuter caravan responds in mass. Last minute lane changes. Accidents. Delays. Commuter fun. The reporter assures Norm that there are no slow downs on 101 this morning.

7:35 380 onto 101 NORTH. Smooth sailing

7:36 380 onto 101 NORTH. Traffic slow**s**

7:39 380 onto 101 NORTH. Complete stop. A three car accident is "working" at the Mission Street exit. Norm has just past the Army exit, his last possible escape from 101. Trapped.

7:45 101 NORTH. Progress = three car lengths. The jam on 101 is four miles long. Norm turns off the radio. A blonde with a fancy hair-cut is sitting in one those new VW's making calls on her cell phone. She has made over fifteen calls since she became Norm's crawl buddy. She looks Norm's way. He gives her one of his patented "what me worry" comic shrugs. She smiles and waves. Life might not be total shit after all.

7:57 101 NORTH. Moving.

8:04 101 NORTH. Stopped.

8:22 Mission exit.. Right onto Bryant. Stop. Traffic not moving in any direction. Going to be late for work again. Damn.

8:39 Besto's Parking. The lot is six blocks from splurch.com and charges $2.00 every twenty minutes. Norm will come back and find a real parking place after he checks into work. He starts to run.

Damn. He is going to have a heart attack right here in the middle of dot comville and nobody will notice or care. Just an old hacker headed off to meet the big programmer in the sky for final de-bugging.

8:48

Norm opens the purple metal splurch.com front door.

"Nice of you to finally show up for work," Milena says as soon as he starts across the floor. below her. "The site has been down for twenty minutes. "

"Going to be an expensive day at the parking lot," mutters Norm to himself as he runs back to his cubicle.

December 20, 1999

Genentech Jumps 158%

SPAM

Monday * December 20, 1999
5:05PM

Splurch.com had installed new blocking software to stop unwanted e-mail. The program also blockied most legitimate incoming e-mail so they removed it. Until the blocking program was fixed and re-installed, all Splurch e-mail accounts were fair game to Spam assaults.

****

SUBJECT: VIAGRA RIGHT TO YOUR DOOR!!
From: lacybamys@popmail.net
Sent: 12/20 4:11 pm
Received: 12/20 4:45 pm
To: UndisclosedRecipients@popmail.net

Breakthrough medication for impotence delivered to your e-mailbox.

Simply Click: http://www.needviagranowww.com

In less than 5 minutes you can complete the on-line consultation and in many cases have the medication in 24 hours.

Simply Click: http://www.needviagranowww.com

From our web site to your e-mailbox. On-line consultation for treatment of compromised sexual function.

Convenient...affordable....confidential.
We ship VIAGRA worldwide at US prices.

To Order Visit: http://www.needviagranowww.com

This is not a SPAM. You are receiving this because you're on a list of email addresses I have bought and you have opted to receive information about business opportunities. If you didn't opt to receive info please accept our apology. To be REMOVED from this list simply reply with REMOVE as subject. And you'll NEVER receive another email from me.

Milena hit **DELETE.**

SUBJECT: MAKE MONEY NOW FOR CHRISTMAS!!!!!!!!
From: sublime303@popmail.net
Sent: 12/20 11:17 am
Received: 12/20 4:47 pm
To: UndisclosedRecipients@popmail.net

If you are tired of working for someone else and are just not appreciated then read on.

We are looking for people with good work ethic and a strong desire to earn $10,000 per month or more right from home.

No experience or special skills required we will give you all the training and support you will need to ensure your success.

This LEGITIMATE HOME BASED INCOME OPPORTUNITY can put you back in control of your life, time, and finances.

Have you tried other opportunitys in the past that have all failed to live up to their promises?

ALL our dreams can come true - if we have the courage to pursue them!!

CALL ONLY IF YOU ARE SERIOUS!!

Milena hit **DELETE.**

****

SUBJECT: SMOKED SALMON, KING CRAB, SHRIMP, AND CAVIAR
From: xyqz45@pol.com
Sent: 12/20 7:11 am
Received: 12/20 4:48 pm
To: vwzq9@pol.com

Give the perfect Christmas gift this Holiday Season. From the cold, wild waters of Alaska we ship world-wide and guarantee delivery of the world's finest and freshest seafood products. We have: Premium Smoked Salmon Huge King Crab   Sweet Shrimp   Gourmet Gift Boxes   Smoked Salmon Caviar. Mention the $5 special when you call and get $5 off your first order.

Happy Holidays:)

Milena hit **DELETE.**

****

SUBJECT: ONE OTHER THING....
From: biz312568@bizmail.com
ReplyTo: bobjaffelen79@yahoo.com
Sent: 12/20 2:11 pm

splurch.com

Received: 12/20 5:50 pm
To: UndisclosedRecipients@bizmail.com

Do you have a Timeshare or Vacation Membership?

Have you thought about renting or selling?

We can help!

For a free consultation simply click reply with your name, address complete telephone number and the name of your Resort.

We will be in touch with you shortly!

Milena hit **DELETE.**

****

SUBJECT: Tired of the 40 X 40 X 40 Plan?
From: tycwdw@pali.com.cn
Sent: 12/18 3:19 am
Received: 12/20 5:01pm
To: UndisclosedRecipients@pali.com.cn

Tired of the 40 X 40 X 40 Plan? You know: Work 40 hours per week for someone else for 40 years, then receive a 40% reduction in pay!

Milena hit **DELETE.**

****

SUBJECT: BUYING A NEW HOME?
From: mortgage367@besmart.com.au@popmail.net
Sent: 12/18 6:01 am
Received: 12/20 5:01 pm
To: Milena_Peterson@splurch.com

<p><FONT face="MS Sans Serif"><p><FONT size=2> <HTML><FONT SIZE=3 PTSIZE=10 FAMILY="SANSSERIF" FACE="Arial" LANG="0">

<p><P ALIGN=CENTER></FONT><FONT COLOR="#ff0000" SIZE=4 PTSIZE=12><B>Are You in Debt? If So, We've Got Some Extremely Good News For You...</FONT><FONT

Milena hit **DELETE.**

****

SUBJECT: You deserve it and its free!!

Milena hit **DELETE.**

****

60

SUBJECT: EARN $200,000 IN 2000

Milena hit **DELETE.**

****

SUBJECT: GUARANTEED way to QUICKLY have EXCELLENT CREDIT!!

Milena hit **DELETE.**

****

SUBJECT: The information you requested.

Milena hit **DELETE.**

****

SUBJECT: Test your investment skills.

Milena hit **DELETE.**

****

SUBJECT: Hi!

Milena hit **DELETE.**

****

SUBJECT: FUCKING FUCK!
From: Tom Samoley [mail to:Tom@SamoleyVentures.com]
Sent: 12/20 5:01 pm
Received: 12/20 5:03 pm
To: Milena_Peterson@splurch.com

EVERYONE on the Board tried to log onto splurch this morning...
they got NOTHING!!!!!

call me

t

THE BOARD

$

Tuesday * December 21, 1999
9:06 AM

Tom smiled broadly at the splurch.com Board of Directors sitting around the gleaming oak table.

"Milena Peterson is now going to come up here and tell us all exactly the kind of profitable future splurch.com is headed for."

Tom sat down next to the large screen filled with the new splurch.com logo, as Milena got up and started through the PowerPoint presentation. Tom tried to focus on what she was saying but it was difficult. He got bored easily. To keep himself in the moment, he started picking crucial points in Milena's presentation and making significant eye contact with the person at the table who might be most interested.

PowerPoint Slide: HIRING FREEZE

MILENA: We are not planning to hire any new employees until after the IPO.

Tom winked at Horace Krennan. Horace winked back and returned to taking copious notes of Milena's presentation.

Horace was a fifty-three year old billionaire from Shaker Heights, Ohio. His father had owned a small business manufacturing engine parts for military aircraft. After he graduated from Ohio State, Horace joined the company and immediately made subtle changes that had profound effects. He shifted the focus from military to civilian - from jet fighters to engine components. Not as glamorous, but steady and extremely profitable. The company ended up building small, esoteric, and expensive consumable engine parts. Horace placed small distribution centers around the country and signed a contract with Federal Express to guarantee delivery of any part anywhere in the world within twenty-four hours. He methodically reviewed his expenses and cut fat whenever it appeared. He sold the business in 1987, moved to Santa

Barbara, and starting investing in computer companies. He became an expert in connecting and keeping track of inventory and the worth of his tech portfolio skyrocketed.

Horace was now worth over three billion dollars. Tom was determined to get some of that cash in his pocket.

PowerPoint Slide: 20% USER INCREASE

MILENA: The number of splurch.com users has grown faster than our original projections.

Tom glanced at Jerry Tenther. Jerry shrugged and turned back to the screen.

Jerry was seventy years old and had been in Silicon Valley from day one. He came up from sales and had survived all the Valley booms and busts. He was a tough love sales manager - an expert at reading contracts and delivering only what the contract said the company would deliver. He was VP of Sales at a major high tech firm when it was acquired by a midwest stock company twenty years ago. He had been cautiously investing his money ever since. He was now worth twenty million dollars.

Jerry was a "weather eye" for the big venture capital firms. His skepticism and careful review of all company contracts made his "thumbs up" a valuable commodity for any new valley company.

Tom wanted to get a "thumbs up" for splurch.com.

PowerPoint Slide: INCOME PROJECTIONS

MILENA: We have identified four new splurch.com markets.

Tom tried to make eye contact with Clarence Wathers III. Clary was leaning back in his chair with his hands laced behind his head - his "I am not buying this" position. Fuck.

Clarence Wathers III was a thirty-one year old Harvard graduate. He went to England as a Rhoades scholar. In England, he had picked up a strong English accent that he still used in his passive-aggressive argumenative style. He got his MBA from Harvard Business and was now desperate to make some kind of big time financial splash. A major Boston based banking firm had hired him to run their venture fund. He made 250K a year just by telling them where they should invest their cash. His "carry" was 12.5% so if the bank made twenty million on one of Clary's investments calls, he took home over three.

Clary Wathers III had his cake and could eat it too.

Tom wanted some of that cake.

PowerPoint Slide: SPLURCH.COM LOGO

MILENA: We have a new logo that we think...

Hernando Formento leaped out of his chair and shouted at Milena, "Who cares about your stupid new logo. I want to know why the site was down yesterday. Five days before Christmas and the site isn't working. Is everyone over there a TOTAL IDIOT?"

Milena froze.

Tom stood up and struggled to quickly come up with the exact right words to explain what went wrong at splurch.com yesterday.

He would earn his money today.

DODGING BULLETS

$

Tuesday * December 21, 1999
9:15 AM

"Hold on Hernando," Tom said as he approached the volatile Cuban and put his arm around his broad shoulders. "Splurch.com is growing quickly. When you grow quickly you have growing pains. Ask any thirteen year old girl."

"Thirteen year old girls don't have millions of dollars invested in a technically screwed up business."

"Not true. I just heard some LA child stars invested in a new dot com this week."

"What company?"

"Don't-grow-ugly-dot-com."

Laughter rippled through the Board room as Hernando's attack on Milena withered.

"Very funny joke Mr. Samoley," said Hernando.

"Why thank you Mr. Formento," said Tom as he patted the venture capitalist on the shoulder. "Now why don't we just wait for Milena to finish her presentation before we start raking her over the coals."

Hernando pulled out a cigar, lit it, and sat back down. Milena returned to her presentation without comment. Hernando had agreed not to smoke at the Board meetings but this didn't seem like the appropriate time to remind him. Besides, to Hernando, cigars weren't smoking. They were the scent of real men.

Out of the corner of his eye, Tom watched Hernando puff away. Hernando Formento was thirty-seven years old. His grandparents had been political allies, business partners and best friends with Fulgencio Batista in pre-communist Cuba. Hernando's grandfather had barely escaped a few weeks before Castro took command of the island. He had been able to liquidate and transfer almost all his Cuban assets to America before fleeing with his family to Florida. He immediately started a series of businesses catering to Cuban American needs. Hernando, his grandson, was wealthy, well educated, and self-important., and drove everyone crazy with his wild mood swings. Hernando ended most of his drinking sessions proclaiming - *I've been groomed to lead. My family will eventually return to Cuba and I'll be elected President.* In his more sober moments, Hernando admitted he would probably only be a member of the Cuban Presidential Cabinet - maybe Secretary of the Treasury.

Tom enjoyed Hernando. He didn't mind quelling the outbursts, and the Cuban's political contacts ran deep.

As Milena neared the end of her presentation, Tom watched the Board members preparing to pounce. He leaned over and whispered into his Assistant's ear, "Is the cake ready, Judy?"

"Yes," she whispered without looking up from her notepad.

"When the logo comes up on the screen go light the candles."

"Okay."

"And come through that door singing Happy Birthday as loud as you can when Milena sits down."

"Okay."

"I really need help today."

"You always need my help Tom."

"And you're always there."

"I am glad you recognize that fact."

The logo appeared and Judy bolted for the door. Tom starting giving Milena "stretch it out" signals. If the Board had a second to start their attack, Tom's birthday ploy wouldn't slow them down. Milena sat down and Judy came bursting through the door.

> *Happy Birthday to you.*
> *Happy Birthday to you.*
> *Happy Birthday dear Jerry*
> *Happy Birthday to you.*

"My birthday isn't 'til next week," Jerry Tenther said as the cake was placed in front of him and he started counting the candles. "And I'm going to be seventy-one - not twenty-one."

"You're only as old as you think you are," said Tom as he stood up behind Jerry.

"Right."

"So today you're twenty-one."

As soon as Judy starting cutting the cake, Hernando shouted, "We have to talk. We can't have the splurch.com web site unavailable all the time..."

The door opened and Staner Lipton came strolling into the room. "Looks like I made it for the best part of the meeting," Staner said as he walked over to the cake, stuck his finger into frosting, and popped a sample into his mouth. "Hmmmm good. Can I have a piece?"

The room exploded in greeting.

Twenty-nine year old Staner Lipton was a star. He had been on the cover of *Wired* twice. He was a boy genius. He was on the splurch.com Board of Directors but rarely showed up for meetings.

The jovial buzz in the room grew stronger as Staner started trading golfing jokes with everyone in the room.

There would be no more talk about splurch.com servers going down at this meeting.

Thank God.

WAY TO SAN JOSE

Wednesday * December 22, 1999
12:39PM

"I'll have a number two."

"Cheese Whoppers are going to kill ya, Holly."

"I don't care, Sal. I like meat and cheese."

"Is that all?" the Burger King box squacked.

"That it, team?" Milena asked her two young passengers.

"If it''s on splurch.com - I'm supersizing," said Holly.

"Noooooo...," screamed Sal from Milena's back seat as he banged his arm cast on his leg cast.

"Sal shut up and eat your little bags of tofu and let me enjoy my life," said Holly as she spun around and stuck her tongue out at the wounded computer genius stretched out on the back seat.

"One Catch of the Sea, one medium diet Dr. Pepper, one number two with a Coke - supersized, and one 2% milk."

"That's right."

"$12.97 at the second window."

"Thanks."

Milena pulled up to the second window. "What did you guys think of the last space we looked at? A lot of room, don't you think?"

"A lot prettier paint than the vomit yellow walls we're looking at every day now," said Holly. "Smells a lot better too. I think once a building is involved in auto parts it will always smell like oil and sweat."

68

"I don't care how pretty, how large, or how good it smells," said Sal, "it's in San Jose and so I hate it."

Milena distributed the food and thought about what a good idea it was to take Holly and Sal on this trip to San Jose. Sal's resistance to the move was slowly evaporating. Time to change the topic.

"Sal, did ya see the story in the morning paper about Y2K?"

"Every story in the morning paper was about Y2K."

"This was the one in the business section about the possibility that hackers are spreading Y2K viruses that will spring to life on January 1st."

"I read it."

"Splurch.com is totally protected from such things, right?"

"Splurch.com is Y2K compliant," Sal chanted. "Our computer clocks will click over to the new millennium with no problem, and we are totally protected from outside viruses."

"Great."

"However..."

"However?"

"I installed a special program on the splurch.com servers just before my unfortunate encounter with that Muni bus."

"What kind of program?"

"Everyone that logs onto the splurch.com home page on January 1st will see a dialogue box with their name, address, and home phone number," said Sal.

Milena gripped the steering wheel. Sal had to be joking.

"Then they'll get transferred to a web page with a picture of the State Bird from the State that they are logging in from," continued Sal.

"Tell her about the people who log in from foreign countries," giggled Holly.

"They'll see pictures of the dragons I drew for our Halloween party," continued Sal. "Most countries don't have official birds."

Don't panic. This was a joke. Milena laughed loudly.

January 1st is a Saturday, so it's perfect." said Holly. "No business people will be logging on and we might generate some great free publicity."

"Build brand awareness," added Sal.

Milena was shaking.

"Then you know what appears?" asked Holly.

"What?" said Milena.

"Milena Peterson's personal e-mail address appears," said Sal.

Sal and Holly both clapped and cheered.

"You believed it," shouted Holly.

"I did not."

"You did for a second," screamed Sal.

"Not even for a second," laughed Milena turning onto 101 and headed towards San Francisco. "Speaking of fun, how's our Holiday Bash shaping up Holly?"

"An evening to remember."

"Everybody coming?"

"Everybody that's in town. Having a Christmas party the day after Christmas turns out to be an insanely good idea. All together now..."

"Thank you Holly," chanted Milena and Sal.

"Is your buddy Phil coming," asked Sal.

"He won't be in San Francisco then," Holly said. "Actually, I am meeting him at the airport tomorrow morning between planes."

Awkward pause.

Milena finally broke the silence, "Speaking of celebrities, Staner Lipton showed up at the Board meeting yesterday."

"Wow," said Holly.

"You have to talk Staner into coming to the office sometime. I want to meet him," said Sal.

"He said he'd come to the office party," said Milena. "But with Staner Lipton you never really know.

Milena's cell rang. She put the phone to her ear.

"Milena, it's Tom."

"Hi Tom.. My partners and I were just scouting our new office digs in San Jose. We..."

"The fucking site is down again!" Tom Samoley barked so loud that everyone in the car could hear the words exploding from Milena's tiny cell phone speaker.

CLICK!

December 22, 1999

Redhat Stock Splits

SPLURCH SERVERS

Wednesday * December 22, 1999
1:17PM

SHIT SHIT SHIT

Norm pounded on his keyboard.

DAMN DAMN DAMN

Norm started typing again. Sweat was pouring from his forehead, and trickling down his back. His stomach was twisting and turning. Hard to believe a human could survive this kind of tension. Four other splurch.com engineers anxiously looked over Norm's shoulder at the screen. No one said a thing. They were out of suggestions. Norm changed numbers, letters, and symbols furiously. Of course. It was simple. Why didn't he think of this before. This would solve the problem. Splurch.com would be back welcoming holiday visitors in minutes.

Everyone held their breath as Norm's latest attempt to get splurch.com back up flew across the fiber to the servers in San Jose.

Done.

Norm switched to Netscape and tried to enter the site. THIS URL CAN NOT BE FOUND appeared again.

Norm checked for the hundredth time to make sure he was trying to log onto splurch.com.

http://www.splurch.com

He hit REFRESH.

PLEASE PLEASE PLEASE

Nothing. The splurch.com home page was still unavailable.

FUCK FUCK FUCK

Norm's cell rang.

"Norm we've been waiting here at baggage for thirty minutes. I thought you were going to pick us up?"

Oh my God thought Norm looking at the clock. He had been planning to come in and work for only a couple of hours and then head to the airport to pick up his brother and sister. All he had to do was make a few small simple changes in the Cron script. Small simple changes. Sure.

"Can you and Sarah just get a cab and meet me at the house?" said Norm furiously trying to rethink the splurch.com problem with most of his brain while using the remaining portion to talk to his brother.

"We can do that but it will be expensive. It's a long way from SFO to San Jose."

"What?"

"It's going to be a costly taxi ride."

"Got you covered bro," said Norm as he started pounding out code again.

"What do we do when we get there?"

"What?"

"When we get to your house. What do we do? Is there a hidden key?"

This would do it. Of course it was simple. How could he have been so stupid. He started moving sections of the code around the screen.

"Norm?"

"What?"

"Is there a hidden key so we can get in your house when we get there."

"Yeah. It's under the flower pot to the right of the door." Norm stopped typing and pounded his forehead. "No it's not. I locked myself out last week and had to use it. I meant to put it back. The key is sitting on the counter right next to the refrigerator."

"Won't do us much good there."

splurch.com

Norm's call waiting started beeping.

"Chris, I got another call, can you wait."

"Sure, we've been waiting for an hour - another few minutes won't hurt."

Norm clicked the phone over to the incoming call and checked Caller ID. Milena Peterson. Damn.

"Norm, why is the site down?"

"It's almost back up."

"When?"

"Real soon."

"When exactly?"

Norm was now perspiring from every pore in his body.

"Thirty minutes."

"Make it fifteen."

"Okay."

"Do you want to talk to Sal?"

"I tried to call him but he wasn't home."

"He's stretched out in the back seat of my car. Would you like to talk to him now

Just what Norm didn't need. Having Sal solve his stupid screw up with Milena listening to every word. Did he have a choice? No.

"Put him on."

In a few minutes, Sal had helped Norm identify the problem. Splurch.com would soon be rolling again. Thank God.

Milena came back on the line.

"Splurch.com will be up, in minutes" said Norm as his body started to relax.

"Good job Norm," said Milena. "Or I should I say good job Sal?"

"It was a team effort."

"Before you leave I want you to change all the passwords."

"That will take a couple of hours."

"We talked about this a week ago. You haven't done it yet and I want it done today."

"Okay."

Milena hung up and Norm clicked to the other line. Dial tone. Shit. His brother and his sister were probably in the taxi and already on the way to his house. They didn't have a cell phone. They didn't have a way to get into his house. Norm wouldn't be able to get home for at least three hours.

Happy Holidays.

December 23, 1999

Amazon CEO Tells Of Life at the Top

SFO

Thursday * December 23, 1999
5:30 AM

"Did I miss anything in Bangalore?"

"A lot of meetings with self important business managers, insecure software engineers and greedy bankers."

"Glad I didn't go."

"You did miss an interesting demonstration of a virtual reality geological computer program," continued Phil. "And too many lonely nights in an empty hotel room."

Holly ignored the lonely room comment.

"Geological virtual reality?"

"It's an application our team in India is creating for oil companies. You load the data that has been accumulated about a geological region into a vector parallel supercomputer. The supercomputer thinks about it for awhile and then projects pictures of the strata on all four walls of the room. You tell the computer operator which direction you want to go - up, down, right, left, forward, or backward. He points the joystick in that direction and you cruise through the earth."

"You're kidding."

"No, I am not. It was fun."

"How does the computer know what's under the ground?"

"The oil company drills for samples, and sets off explosions to monitor the sound echoes just like they've always done. When they accumulate enough information, geologists used to take the data, interpret it, and draw maps of what it probably looks like under the surface. With our new program, however, all they have to do is feed the raw data into the computer and start traveling through the ground looking for oil."

"Does it work?"

Phil laughed. "It's a brand new computer program. Sometimes it works but most of the time it doesn't."

"Did you get stuck under the earth?"

"A lot. Mainly because the program designer was sick the day of the demonstration and the person doing it couldn't quite figure out how to get our rock rocket rolling. The other problem was that most of the computer brain running the software was tied up executing another program at the same time. We traveled through rocks - but real slow."

"That would have been fun to see."

"I wish you'd been there."

Holly and Phil sat in silence on the couch in the Red Carpet Lounge and watched the room fill up with early morning first class holiday flyers.

"It was sure nice of you to get up in the middle of the night to meet me here at the airport."

"I don't need sleep," Holly joked. "I stopped sleeping months ago. I think the last time I slept was at the University of San Francisco - my Advanced Statistics lecture."

"I owe you."

"Big time."

Phil took a deep breath. "I am flying back to San Francisco next week and my parents are having a small New Year's eve Y2K party at the Fairmont Hotel. I was wondering if you want to be there."

"Meet your parents?"

"Yeah."

"A date type thing?"

"Yeah."

"Okay."

"Great," said Phil as he reached into his briefcase and pulled out a small box wrapped in bright reindeer paper and adorned with a shiny gold bow. "I got you a present in India."

Holly looked at that little box sitting in Phil's hand. "You're giving me a Christmas present? I didn't get you anything."

"It's not a Christmas present. It's just something that I saw at one of the shops in the Bangalore hotel lobby that I thought you'd like. And you already gave me a Christmas gift - you got up in the middle of the night and drove to the San Francisco airport to chat for twenty minutes with lonely old Phil."

Holly opened the box. A diamond encrusted elephant with bright ruby eyes gleamed up at her.

Phil took the elephant out of the box and pinned it on Holly's sweater. He leaned back and looked at the sparkling pin on her left breast - inches from her heart "Looks great."

Holly looked down at the expensive gift and when she looked up, Phil's lips were approaching hers. As soon as their lips met, Phil's tongue shot through her parted teeth and started exploring.

Oh man.

Phil removed his tongue and slowly their lips parted. He looked at his watch.

"Better roll. I'll call you as soon as I get back."

Phil grabbed his briefcase and raced out of the lounge.

As soon as Phil disappeared, Holly remembered she had promised Sal she would get together with him on New Year's Eve to watch the world crumble.

No problem. Sal would understand. He was that kind of guy.

SMOKE

Friday * December 24, 1999
1:30 PM

Milena was working in her loft command center - one eye on the computer screen and one eye on the purple metal door at the far end of the former auto part warehouse that was now the home of splurch.com.

Every time another brave employee decided it was Christmas Eve and okay to leave early, Milena would shout a hearty MERRY CHRISTMAS and ask if that employee was planning to make it to the office Christmas party on Sunday. Everyone explained the reason that they *absolutely positively* had to leave the office early and assured her that they would be at the party.

Milena tried not to judge her employees by the time they left the office on Christmas eve. She wasn't a Scrooge. This was the new economy. New rules. It didn't matter what time an employee came into the office or what time they left. The thing that mattered was the quality of the work they did. If an employee wanted to work from midnight to dawn - that was okay. If an employee wanted to come to work wearing only buckskin and a coonskin cap - or wrapped in a batman cape - or dressed in a large pink bunny suit - that was okay. The only thing that her employees should be judged on was the quality of their work.

Sure.

Reality: Milena's best employees came into the office early and left late. For the most part, they dressed normally and were easy to get along with.

More Reality: Every employee that had deserted her team so far was already on Milena's list of the people who would be let go the next time that the Board of Directors demanded she reduce the splurch.com burn rate.

The more things changed the more they stayed the same.

"Merry Christmas Norm!"

"Merry Christmas Milena," said Norm as he looked up with the broadest smile he could manage. "I have to get home and spend time with my brother and sister. They've been sitting at my house all day without a car. Imagine trying to do anything in San Jose without a car."

"Kind of like being without a car in Los Angeles."

"Right."

"Coming to the party Sunday?"

"You bet. Is it okay if I bring my brother and sister?"

"Sure. The more the merrier." Milena bit her lip. Holly had asked every employee two weeks ago how many people they wanted to bring to the party so the right amount of food and drink could be ordered. Typical Norm Fuck Up.

"My brother and sister ended up sitting on my front porch for three hours yesterday while I was here trying to get our servers up and running. I figure we owe 'em some food and drink."

"They're invited," said Milena cheerily as she seethed inside. It was Norm's fault that he had to stay late. YOU IDIOT! If he hadn't tried to make that stupid improvement on the web site he would have been done in plenty of time to go pick up his idiot relatives.

"The reason I am leaving early is because I promised them we would visit the San Jose Museum of Science and Technology today. They're from Boston. He works for DEC and she works at the Museum of Art. I thought going to The Tech together would be fun."

"The Tech isn't going to be open."

"Yes they are. They are open 'til 8 pm on Fridays."

"Norm, it's Christmas eve. They aren't going to be open."

Norm stood smiling up at Milena.

"You're probably right," he finally said. "But we're going to give it a try."

Norm disappeared and Milena thought about how high Norm would be on her firing list if Sal Zaldivar wasn't out of commission and IT computer experts weren't so hard to come by.

"Are we ready for our afternoon coffee break?" Holly shouted as she pushed back from her computer station on the far side of the loft.

"Sure.

Holly started skipping down the circular staircase, stopped, and sniffed. "Do you smell anything?"

Milena sniffed. "No."

"Try over here."

Milena crossed to the circular stairs and sniffed. "Smoke."

"Yeah - smoke."

Milena and Holly looked up. The warehouse ceiling was disappearing under a thin cloud of dirty white smoke. More smoke was pouring through the small windows that lined the wall just below the roof.

They two women watched in horror as the cloud of smoke grew black and doubled in size.

They both screamed.

"FIRE!"

FIRE

Friday * December 24, 1999
1:45 PM

Flames shot over two hundred feet in the air.

Holly had never seen a fire like this.

Holly was on the far side of Bryant with the splurch.com employees and all the other SOMA dot com workers that hadn't left work early for Christmas eve. They all watched as the unoccupied building five doors down from splurch.com slowly turned into a roaring inferno. The size and fury of the angry flames was terrifying. The volume of noise coming from the blaze was even more frightening. The constant roar of wind and flames was punctuated by continual pops of exploding paint cans and the crack of burning wooden beams. Screaming sirens, clanking alarms, and the shouts of arriving San Francisco police officers filled out the wall of sound.

Milena called Tom Samoley on her cell phone.

"We have a fire."

Milena covered the phone with both hands to hear Tom's response over the roar of the blaze.

"It's not us. It's five doors down. That empty paint place," Milena shouted into her cell.

Three fire trucks converged on the burning building.

"Yeah. Everybody is out of splurch.com."

Firemen hooked hoses to hydrants and two pumper trucks began pouring water onto the buildings on either side of the raging inferno.

"I don't think we're in any immediate fire danger," Milena shouted into the phone.

Water hit the flames and the volume of smoke doubled. A swirling grey cloud slowly erased the yellow brick splurch.com building from view.

"We might have smoke damage," shouted Milena.

Patrol cars and fire trucks were now pouring in from both ends of Bryant.

Milena pulled the cell from her ear and turned to Holly and shouted, "Tom was at a fund raiser at the Civic Center with Willie Brown. They're both on their way."

"Everybody loves a fire.," Holly shouted back..

"Call Norm and get him back here. Tom wants to figure out what to do about protecting the computers from smoke."

Holly took Milena's cell phone and called Norm.

"Hey Norm. Want to come back to work?"

Holly removed the phone from her ear and waited for Norm to finish his tirade and then calmly started talking again.

"I know it's fucking Christmas Eve, and I know your fucking brother and sister are visiting, and I know you haven't spent any fucking time with them buttttt... a large fire is cooking a building five doors from splurch.com right now and you have to come back."

Norm agreed to return.

"See ya soon," Holly said into the cell before handing it back to Milena. "On his way."

"Good job."

The KRON television crew arrived. A reporter leaped out of the truck with a large phallic antenna on the roof and approached a smiling Milena. "You know what happened?"

"Sort of."

"Want to do an interview?"

"Sure."

Milena joked about how many times she could mention splurch.com as the cameraman set up a camera shot with the flaming building in the background. A shiny silver stretch limo pulled in front of the burning building. Willie Brown climbed out followed by Tom Samoley. The TV reporter and cameraman immediately abandoned Milena and headed towards "Da Mayor."

Tom started crossing the street towards splurch.com. "Milena come with me. You too Holly."

A large burly Irish cop grabbed Tom before he got half way across the street.

"Where are you going buddy?"

"I have to get some stuff out of that building."

"You can't do that now."

"It's my building. I own it."

"In case you haven't noticed, a building is on fire."

"It's five buildings down. I just have to get some computer equipment out of my building."

"I'll let you know when you can do that," said the policeman as he escorted Tom back across the street and herded him under the bright yellow police tape that was now strung between all the parking meters.

Tom saw Norm approach and yelled. "Is that smoke going to hurt our computers?"

Norm stared at him slack jawed.

"What?"

"How do we protect our computers from that smoke?"

"I don't know."

"THEN FIND OUT!" Tom screamed as he headed towards the Mayor's limo to see if he could find some higher powers to aid his attempt to remove his computer equipment from the splurch.com office.

Norm pulled out his cell and handed it to Holly. "Do you know Sal's home number?"

Holly punched in the numbers and Sal came on immediately.

"Sal. What are ya doin' for fun?"

"Trying to watch televison, but some stupid fire is on every station," Sal said.

"That's right. Nothing like a seven alarm fire to interrupt your regular television programming."

Holly looked at the sea of cameras that were now set up along Bryant broadcasting pictures of the SOMA fire to the world.

"Alright Sal, I am passing you to Norm so you can chat about computers and smoke."

What a delightful Christmas Eve, Holly thought as she handed the cell to Norm.

> *Buildings roasting in an open fire.*
> *Tom Samoley biting at our nose.*

December 24, 1999

Y2K Scare

MERRY CHRISTMAS

Saturday * December 25, 1999
1:23 PM

Sal used his uncasted left hand to move the cursor to the NORTON UTILITIES icon in the the upper right corner of the grimy I-MAC screen. He clicked, and a list of the applications appeared. Sal checked through the list to make sure he had tested all the applications that were normally used on this computer. He moved the cursor down the list until the computer icon and FINDER were framed by a black bar. He released the button and moved to SPECIAL on the top row of the smoke covered computer screen. He moved down the list until SHUT DOWN was highlighted, and released the button.

"NUMBER TWENTY OKAY," shouted Sal across the splurch.com office space.

"Hooray," cheered Holly from the front of the former auto parts warehouse where she was wiping away smoke grime and restoring the yellow brick walls to their pre-fire ugliness.

"You are THE MAN," shouted Milena from her Executive Loft. Milena was on the phone slowly making her way through a list of splurch.com employees to inform them that -

1. The "day after Christmas" Sunday office party was canceled.

2. Everyone should come to work on Monday.

Sal stepped into the next cubicle. The splurch.com offices had been filled with smoke for at least four hours. Most of the CD-ROM optical sensors were destroyed but, so far, only two of the computers had any other major problems. Sal actually wasn't sure if those problems were smoke related or pre-fire operator error. I-Macs are pretty resilient machines, he thought as he watched number twenty-one boot up.

Even though it was Christmas Day, Sal was happy to be doing something useful. His broken right arm was turning into a big time pain. Since he wasn't able to program or do any graphic work, he was getting more and more frustrated. For years, he had worked all the time. He was happy when he was working and this was working. Sort of.

Sal put a pencil in his mouth so he could hit two computer keys simultaneously and Holly came weaving into the cubicle.

"Sal you must save me," she said as she leaned on the metal office desk gasping for air. "The smoke is killing me. The awful smell has made its way to my brain core. I can't breathe. I can't take it any morrrrrrrre."

Holly collapsed to the floor.

"Save me Sal," she whispered before groaning and pretending to drift into unconsciousness.

Sal leaned over Holly's body. "How can I save Holly?"

Holly mumbled, "Sal will save me. I can count on Sal."

Sal leaned closer. Holly's face was now totally void of expression. She was so pretty. So alive. So much fun. So dating a dot com millionaire.

"How can Sal save Holly," Sal whispered in her ear.

"He can take Holly out of this smelly smelly place. He can take her to have lunch someplace where it doesn't stink."

"Sal can do that."

"Great." Holly leaped to her feet. "Fresh air here we come."

Holly told Milena that they would return shortly and they headed out to find a place to lunch on Christmas Day.

It didn't take long to find an open restaurant. A multitude of cultures had established South of Market beach heads and December 25th was not a holiday for most of them.

"I was expecting out of this world appetizers," said Holly as she took another bite of her Great Crab in Black Bean Sauce. "This restaurant is supposed to have the best food in the world, right?"

"I've never been here so I wouldn't know."

"It's a San Francisco restaurant. It's got to be great to survive."

Holly had been giving Sal a blow by blow account of one of her dining adventures with zillionaire Phil. Every time she started on the subject, Sal smiled but his insides screamed in pain. He was now Holly's best friend. Great. He laughed at a joke about the black velvet Elvis painting in the last restaurant Phil took her.

He should tell Holly how he really felt. And he would tell her. Someday.

Sure.

"What's happening with the insurance thing?" Holly asked.

"According to the hospital I owe them over a hundred thousand dollars," Sal said as he took a sip of green tea. "I've asked Milena about it a couple of times but she says not too worry. It will get worked out."

"So it will get worked out."

"I hope so. I don't have a hundred grand sitting in my Swiss bank account. "

"Close?"

"If ya count all my diamonds and gold shoe laces."

"I don't think the hospital will accept diamonds and gold shoe laces as payment."

"Probably not."

December 20, 1999

NASDAQ Flirts with 4,000

WARRIORS

$

Monday * December 27, 1999
8:56 PM

2:05 left in the third.

Win one for Gerry.

The Warriors trailed the World Champion San Antonio Spurs by five points. The home town b-ballers had come back from fourteen down.

Win one for Gerry.

Tom had court-side seats for the game. He and thousands of fans who had shown up at the Oakland Coliseum the day after Christmas to support the struggling Bay Area professional basketball franchise They were now standing and screaming for John Starks, Terry Cummings, Donnyell Marshall, Antawn Jamison, and the rest of the under-manned and over-injured Warriors to...

Win one for Gerry.

Time Out Spurs.

Tom exchanged high fives with Horace Krennan, and spun around to low five Hernando Formento. Hernando was waving his arms in the air and screaming WARRIORS. As soon as he saw the two offered palms, Hernando brought his hands down on Tom's with a loud smack. Clary Wathers III - the third splurch.com board member Tom had invited to this game - remained in his seat but was clapping in rhythm with the chanting crowd.

Win one for Gerry.

This was the perfect opportunity to bring up difficult splurch.com business. Simple psychology. Everyone loved a winner. It was going to be a lot easier talking his seatmates into increasing their splurch.com investment when the smell of winning filled the air.

Six months ago, Tom had sat down next to Gerry St. Jean at a Warrior charity luncheon and joked about the upcoming basketball season. Gerry told Tom that when he was head coach, he would give Tom front row seats for the first game. They continued to joke for the entire luncheon about Tom's free tickets for Gerry's first game as head coach. Neither man had any idea that by Christmas Day the Warriors would be 6 - 21 and that P.J. Carlesimo - forever branded as the coach who choked Latrell Sprewell - would be out the door.

Less than four hours before the game, the Warriors fired Carlesimo and announced that Gerry St. Jean would take over the head coaching responsibilites. Tom immediately called the Warriors' office to congratulate Gerry and jokingly remind him of the July luncheon commitment. To his surprise, someone from the Warriors called back an hour later to say that there would be four court side tickets waiting at the Will Call window for Samoley Ventures.

Tom started calling the splurch.com Board of Directors. Jerry Tenthor claimed that his wife wouldn't let him out of the house between Christmas and New Years but Horace and Hernando both jumped at free courtside Warrior tickets and Clary decided he might be willing to mix with the proletariat for at least one evening.

Tom's father, John, had shown Tom how to use sports events to convince people to do things they would never do in a sterile office. He had bought a Dallas Cowboy sky box. He charged it to his advertising budget, and invited video store and chain owners from all over the country to the games. He filled his guests with food and liquor, and during Cowboy victory celebrations talked them into all sorts of business deals.

Time In.

The Warriors and Spurs returned to the floor. Tom decided to wait until the end of the quarter to casually bring up the splurch.com need for additional financing.

David Robinson - the seven foot Spur captain - threw down a dunk, and the volume of the Warrior cheering decreased.

John Starks shot an air ball, the Spurs raced down the floor scored, again, and the crowd got quieter.

The Warriors threw the ball away and the Spurs scored again.

The quarter ended, and Tom looked at his chair mates. Horace and Hernando were now quietly sipping their beers. Clary had lost all interest in the game and was now peering at the bouncing breasts of a cheerleader dancing only a few feet away.

If the Warriors made a come back in the fourth quarter, Tom would bring up the splurch.com need for additional investment.

It didn't happen. The Spurs scored sixteen unanswered points and the Warriors had their 22nd loss of the season.

Tom was planning to introduce everyone to Gerry St. James after the game. Easy to do if the Warriors had won. Impossible now.

The disgruntled crowd filed out of the Coliseum. Tom's opportunity to casually discuss splurch.com's cash flow problems and possible financing solutions had past.

Oh well.

Ya win some. Ya lose some.

THE TECH

Tuesday * December 28, 1999
10:47 AM

"I am not going in."

"What are you talking about," Norman said to his brother Chris as they waited for the doors to open at The San Jose Technology Museum of Innovation. "We have been planning on visiting this museum ever since you and Sarah said you were coming to California for Christmas."

"I've already seen everything they've got in there," said Chris. "So why don't you two go in. I'll just sit and have coffee and a donut here at the Cafe Primavera."

"That's totally stupid." Norm said. He had forgotten how ridiculous his older brother could sometimes be.

"I've already seen everything in there ON-LINE anyway."

"What?"

"I was stuck in your house with absolutely nothing to do, no car to go anywhere, no food in the refrigerator, no..."

Sarah started playfully pounding Chris with a plastic map of the Bay Area that she had been carrying ever since she got off the plane. "Stop Christopher Dotoshay. YOU STOP IT RIGHT NOW!"

"Why should I stop? For years Norm has been begging us to come visit him in California and then when we finally fly all the way from Boston, he parks us at his house and leaves us alone for three days."

"Chris. There was a fire at splurch.com. It was an emergency," Sarah said.

"What about Norm's pre-emergency hospitality. What about making his brother and sister wait on his front step of his house for three hours when we first got here? Or what about making us pay for a taxi instead of coming to pick us up at the airport like any normal brother would do?"

"I offered to pay for the taxi," said Norm.

"We don't want any of your dot com dollars," said Chris wagging his finger at Norm. "I have already seen everything they have in that stupid California innovation museum. I saw it on-line. I don't need to see it in reality."

"You are a total idiot Chris," Norm said, "A totally insane idiot."

Sarah started pummeling Chris and Norm with her plastic map. "Stop it. Stop it. Stop it.".

"I've been doing real work for a real computer company for twenty years," Chris shouted back. "I haven't been dreaming up computer fantasies twenty-four hours a day since the ninth grade like my little brother Norm. I didn't spend the last twenty years doing twenty different jobs at twenty different companies, and getting Mom and Dad to bail me out every time his next BIG COMPUTER THING fell flat on it's face."

"That was a shitty think to say." Norm yelled as he poked Chris with his finger.. "You are jealous because I take chances. You've never taken a chance in your life. You are jealous because I do interesting computer problem solving work every day. You work for an old dead computer company that hasn't had an original idea in a hundred years. You put numbers into two different columns and at the end of the day hope they add up."

"DEC is not an old dead computer company. We make money every quarter. WE MAKE MONEY EVERY DAY!" Chris shouted.

The other people in line fidgeted and hoped that the two fifty-year olds were just joking with each other.

Sarah grabbed Chris' ear with one hand and Norm's ear with the other and pulled them both towards the museum door. "Family Feud over. Time to visit the The Tech."

As soon as the Dotoshays entered the museum, their sibling fighting ended. The Tech was filled with fun for kids of all ages and the three overgrown adolescents had a fantastic time playing with the multitude of creative exhibits.

At the big Silicon Wafers, Norm's hands fit into the prints of Bill Hewlett, Chris' into Dave Packard's, and Sarah's into Steve Wozniak's. The brothers voted Sarah the winner.

At the Space Exhibit, the Dotoshays picked the right orbital equipment rack for their space rocket and had a successful space docking experience. They never stopped screaming on the virtual roller coaster and, once they survived the 1989 Loma Prieta, were completly hooked on the quake exhibit. They tried every vibration it offered - twice.

Norm had been meaning to visit The Tech forever, but he had never found the time to go. Even if he had found the time, he probably wouldn't have had anyone to go with him. He was sure his cats weren't interested in visiting the Human Experience Exhibit.

At 5 PM the museum closed and the guard ordered the Dotoshays to leave.

Norm decided he was going to get Chris and Sarah jobs at splurch.com and make them both move to the Bay Area. It was time they joined the dot com revolution.

December 28, 1999

San Francisco a Monetary Mecca

RITE SPOT

Tuesday * December 28, 1999
11:39 PM

"There are two kinds of money," Milena shouted over the din at the Rite Spot on Folsom and 16th.

"There are way more than two kinds of money," Addy Lister yelled back. "Paper money, plastic money, metal money, monopoly money, rubles, copecs, the little numbers that appear on the ATM window when ya try to make a withdrawal and don't have sufficient funds, poker chips, subway tokens..."

"ADDY SHUT UP," Milena reached over the table and put a hand over her best friend's mouth. "Let me get through this. PLEASE."

Addy raised her arms in mock surrender and bumped the small table between them. The burning candle and two Vodka Gimlets slid across the sparkling white table cloth towards the table edge. Addy grabbed both drinks but let the candle crash to the floor.

"Both mine now!" Addy said as Milena reached down to pick up the burning candle rolling past her feet.

"I'll order two more," said Milena.

"You do that girl," Addy shouted as Milena headed towards the wooden bar that dominated the eclectic SOMA night spot. "This could be our last chance to party before the end of the world. ALL those computers are going to click to zero, the power grid is going to shut down, planes will crash, and anarchy will reign. It will THEN be almost IMPOSSIBLE to get a decent Gimlet."

Milena waited with the crowd at the bar. On her right a forty some-thing dressed in a three piece suit and wearing a snappy Fedora (writer?) joked with an aqua haired twenty-something with a pierced tongue (video game tester?). Every time the Hunk Bartender behind the bar passed, Milena tried to catch his eye with a smile. Obviously,

95

Hunk had a system and wasn't going to deviate. Fifteen years ago, her smile would have made him deviate. Oh well.

Milena's cell rang. She checked caller ID. Tom Samoley. Shit.

"Hello."

Milena could hear Tom but his words were total mush.

"I can't hear you Tom. I'll have to take the phone outside."

Milena started towards the front door. She stepped into the chilly San Francisco night and took a couple of gulps of fresh air to reduce her inebriation level. She waited as two low riders with blaring sound systems rolled down Fulton and made the turn on 16th towards Mission.

Milena put the phone to her ear. All she got was a dial tone. She hit Samoley on the speed dial.

Ten rings. No answer.

Typical Tom.

Milena decided it would be a better to talk with Tom in the clear light of day anyway. She headed back into the Rite Spot.

"Who called?"

"Samoley."

"Milena. Listen to me. You have to turn your cell phone off at nine o'clock - EVERY NIGHT. Your cell phone is a leash that old Tommy boy can tug whenever he feels like it."

"I know."

"Turn it off right now."

Milena did.

"Now take a drink and tell me about the two kinds of money."

Milena looked down at the table where a new drink awaited. She took a sip and held up one finger.

"The first kind of money is the kind you have in your pocket. It's real. You know exactly what you can buy with it."

Milena held up two fingers.

"The second kind of money is company money. Like splurch.com money. It's unreal. It's just numbers. We put the numbers into one budget column and then move them into another. It's just endless digits to worry about, and not let drop to zero."

Addy looked at Milena and finally said, "That doesn't make any sense."

Milena shook her head in agreement. "I know. It sounded totally reasonable in my head but when I got half way through telling you I realized how ridiculous it sounded."

"You think about money too much."

"That's all I think about. And worry about. And dream about."

"Is splurch.com having money problems?"

"Did you cash the check for your work on our logo yet?"

"Yes."

"Good," said Milena as she drained her drink. "I hope it's just a temporary money problem. But ya never know."

"Money talk over," said Addy. "Let's talk men."

"Good idea."

Milena and Addy spent another hour talking men at the Rite Spot.

When Milena got home, her answering machine was flashing.

"This is Tom. Why did you turn off your cell? Call me immediately. It doesn't matter what time it is. Our cash flow problem just got worse. A lot worse."

Milena stared at the answering machine for almost a minute. She sighed, picked up the receiver, and started dialing Tom Samoley.

DIVORCE

$

Wednesday * December 29, 1999
1:47 PM

Tom picked up the phone half way through the first ring.

"Why did you turn off your cell?" he barked.

As Milena began explaining her need for free time from her CEO responsibilities, Tom took another sip of Scotch, leaned back in his deck chair, and stared bleary eyed at the reflection of the moon on the water of his Olympic-size swimming pool.

Tom cut Milena off in the middle of her apology speech.

"I got the divorce settlement today." He drained the rest of the drink and threw the glass into the pool. It hit the water with a dramatic splash, and slowly sank to the bottom. Tom waited until the waves from the splash had totally vanished. "The judgement was a total disaster. The judge fully vested her founders' stock even though she sure as hell didn't earn any of it through sweat equity. He ended up giving the bitch five times what she deserved."

Milena began a sympathy speech, and Tom raised the half drained bottle of Dewars to his lips and took a long pull. When he had heard enough of Milena's empathetic babblings he cut her off again.

"Milena you were right. I should never have married that gold miner. I should have married you."

Silence.

Tom took another swig of scotch and let the silence linger. Tom met Milena ten years ago at a Comdex software convention in Las Vegas. She was Director of Marketing for Intellex and was pushing a new accounting program called Bottom Line. Bottom Line was the hottest product at the convention. Tom was looking for new all purpose accounting software for the Samoley video stores. He set

98

up an appointment with Milena for a demo and was enthralled by her energy, enthusiasm, and wide-ranging grasp of the accounting problems. He invited her to dinner the next night to discuss details of a possible Samoley purchase of Bottom Line software for all 347 of their retail outlets. Tom went all out. He got a private dining room at the Mirage and had catered dishes brought in from several different kinds of restaurants. During dessert, he agreed to purchase the Bottom Line software and shook Milena's hand. After dinner, they went dancing to celebrate at a honky tonk Tom had discovered on the outskirts of Vegas during one of his numerous college jaunts to this gambling center of the universe. They returned to his penthouse suite at the Mirage for a nightcap. After the nightcap, they climbed into bed.

Milena finally broke the silence.

"Why did you say that Tom?"

"I am sorry. I am loaded, depressed, and a total asshole. I know that we decided a long time ago that there was no romance in our future but every once in awhile..."

Another silence.

"I am never going to fall in love again. I swear. I am through chasing skirts. I am through with marriage. I am just going to concentrate on what I am good at. Making money."

"Good idea."

"Maybe I'll switch to men. San Francisco is the center of the gay universe. I should take advantage of that fact. There must be a zillion men who would be perfect for me. I bet having a relationship with a man would be a lot less brain damaging than trying to deal with the insane women I have been chaining myself too."

"I don't think a romantic relationship with a man would be any less brain damaging."

"You're probably right."

"And I am fairly sure that you are 100% hetero. I don't think it's something you have a lot of choice over."

"I suppose you're right about that too."

splurch.com

Another silence.

Tom walked out onto his diving board and started bouncing.

"Here's the problem. The divorce is going to seriously crimp my cash flow. I won't know how much "til I talk to my accountant. I think it will effect us. The money I was going to throw into splurch.com this month might not be there. I couldn't get any of our investors to cough up more dough at the Warrior game, so we might have a cash crunch in the not too distant future."

"Will it effect the IPO."

"Don't know yet. We should have done a mezzanine funding round." Tom bounced higher and higher. "I was too optimistic about this fucking divorce settlement."

"What are we going to do?"

"Start looking for cash. Now."

Tom bounced off the board into the pool.

SPLASH!

December 29, 1999

U.S. Licks Y2K Bug

TEA GARDEN

Wednesday * December 29, 1999
2:11 PM

"They shouldn't have charged you."

"Why?"

"Everyone in a cast should get free admission."

"Is that part of the Holly Health Insurance Program."

"One of the most important benefits," said Holly as she spread the green and gold University of San Francisco blanket on the lawn next to the pond with the giant gold fish.

Milena had given Holly the keys to her Mercedes and told her to leave work early and take Sal on a picnic in Golden Gate Park. They had driven to Stow Lake with plans to rent a rowboat, but when they got there, Sal realized that with only one leg and one arm free - if he fell in the water even though it was only three feet deep - he would probably drown. They decided to picnic at the Japanese Tea Garden instead of rowing across Stowe Lake.

Sal was now passing out Calistogas and avocado and cream cheese sandwiches. "The problem with your health plan is that people would make fake casts so they could get into places like this for free."

"Every gate would have an x-ray machine to make sure that you really had something broken before they let you in free."

"All those x-rays would be bad for people's health."

"You must be a Republican."

"I am a nothing. I've never voted in my life."

"Figured." Holly took a bite out of her sandwich. "No interest in enlightened public policies."

101

Sal and Holly ate and watched an endless parade of tourists crossing the bridge spanning the gold fish pond.

"My landlady said admission to the Tea Garden used to be free."

"Back when cable cars were a nickel?"

"Before San Francisco realized it was an adult Disneyland and you could charge tourists outrageous sums for anything they did while they were here."

"Everything in the Park should be free for San Francisco residents."

"Agreed."

"How do you check who's a resident and who's not?"

"Use the x-ray machines. Once you've lived in San Francisco for over a year, your internal structure changes."

"Of course."

Holly and Sal finished their sandwiches and lay back on the blanket watching the fog roll in over the eucalyptus trees swaying in the breeze.

"Tell me how the world is going to end Friday," Holly said dreamily.

"Many many years ago a band of evil programmers set the clocks inside our computers for disaster. When the computer clocks try to change from December 31, 1999 to January 1, 2000 they will change to January 1, 1900 instead.

"Will all the planes fall from the sky?"

"Of course. Plane will not have been invented yet, so how can they fly? Power plants will think they need maintenance and will all shut down."

"Will phones work?"

"Of course not. But telegraphs will. That's why I learned Morse code in the hospital."

"Can you teach me?"

"Dot dash is A."

"Dot dash is A. Okay"

"Dot dash dot dot is B."

"Too hard. Just teach me SOS."

"Dot dot dot dash dash dash dot dot dot."

"Dot dot dot dash dash dash dot dot dot," Holly repeated.

Sal immediately stood on his one good foot and saluted. "I got your SOS ma'am. Can I be of help? "

Holly answered in her best damsel in distress voice. "Oh good sir. The world is going to end this weekend. Will you save me?"

"Yes I will."

They both laughed and then Holly said, "There won't be any real problems will there?"

"If you asked me that a year ago, I would have said we were headed for disaster. It appears, however, that everybody has worked long and hard enough so things will be okay."

"That's good."

"But you can't be sure," said Sal as he lay back down on the blanket and watched the dancing tree branches. "Computers are full of unknowns and they have a tendency to breakdown at the worst possible time so who knows?"

"Have you got a supply of dried food, flashlights, and batteries ready?"

"I also have a secret tunnel under my apartment to hide during the chaos. You are welcome to join me on Friday night."

"It's a date," Holly laughed.

"Tonight I'll start making the tunnel big enough for two."

Holly clapped her hands. "Damn. I forgot. I am meeting Phil's parents at the Fairmont on Friday night. We'll have to wait until the day after the end of the world to get together."

Sal sighed as he watched the sea gulls dance through the fog. That's right, he thought, Holly will take the cripple on a mercy picnic but she won't go out with him until the day after the end of the world.

SPLURCH TOUR

🔒

Friday * December 31, 1999
9:37 AM

"Milena is tough."

"Tough as nails?" asked Norm's brother Chris from the shotgun seat.

"Tough as ground-in-dirt?" asked his sister Sarah from the back.

"Tough as the Three Tenors?" continued Chris.

"Three Tenors? What are you talking about?" laughed Norm as he headed down the ramp and took a right onto Bryant. Great, he thought. No traffic. Everybody must have evacuated the city to seek shelter in Nevada caves in preparation for tonight's millennium chaos.

"Chris hates the Three Tenors," laughed Sarah. "The hundredth time they came on PBS he screamed in pain."

"Those guys have overstayed their public television welcome," said Chris. "As long as they're on, I will no longer contribute to my local public television station."

"You won't have to contribute to PBS for awhile then," said Norm as he drove past a strange sight - available street parking on Bryant. "The Three Tenors are permanent public television fixtures."

"Like those distinguished men and woman who show up in their sincere suits begging for money every three months," said Sarah.

"The public television station managers?" asked Norm.

"Yeah. They all ought to be taken out behind the barn and put out of their misery," said Sarah.

Norm pulled into a parking spot across the street from the charred remnants of the building five doors down from splurch.com.

"Wow" Chris said pointing at the blackened frame of the former paint warehouse. "That must have been fun to watch."

"It was," said Norm.

"Any effect on splurch.com?" asked Sarah.

"It appears our computers survived with no problem."

"Your computers are tough." said Chris.

"Tough as nails," sang Sarah as the three siblings headed up Bryant together.

"Tough as ground-in-dirt," shouted Chris.

"Tough as the Three Tenors," laughed Norm as they reached the purple door with the cardboard sign announcing splurch.com in block letters. "It still smells like smoke though."

Norm opened the door and Chris and Sarah immediately wrinkled their noses. "Mmmmmm...," said Chris. "My favorite smell. Barbecued warehouse."

Holly was skipping down the red circular staircase with an armful of files. She immediately shouted, "Norm! You brought your posse to work with ya."

"Right," said Norm. "Chris and Sarah, this is Holly Chen. Holly is the winner of the most enthusiastic Splurch.com employee award for three months running."

"GO SPLURCH!" said Holly as she improved a little splurch.com dance. "Norm says you guys are from the East Coast."

"We are," said Chris.

"When are you planning to leave that land of desolation and cold and come live with us in the land of opportunity and sun?"

"As soon as Norm gets us jobs," said Sarah.

"Computer people?" asked Holly.

"Yes," said Sarah.

"Splurch.com can always use more good computer people. You're hired."

"When did Milena put you in charge of hiring?" said Norm as he punched Holly playfully on the arm.

"Darn. That's right," said Holly covering her face with the files. "I don't start that job 'til next week. How embarrassing. Could you two wait until then to start your new jobs?"

"Sure," said Chris.

"Where is the Commander-in-Chief?" asked Norm.

"Hasn't come in yet," said Holly. "And hasn't called. Strange. But here at dot com land every day is a new adventure and I expect I'll be hearing from her about our latest splurch.com crisis soon.

"I am not an engineer today," said Norm. "I am a San Francisco tour guide and I am starting the tour with a visit to splurch.com - the best dot com in the universe."

"Sounds like fun," said Holly as she waved the files and headed towards the copier.

As Norm started pointing out splurch.com points of interest, Milena came marching in the front door. The cloud of tension and gloom surrounding her was almost visible.

"Milena I would like you to meet my brother and sister, Christopher and Sarah Dotoshay," said Norm.

"How do you do?" said Milena. "Norm could I talk to you for a second?"

"Sure."

"In the loft."

"Okay."

Milena crossed the floor and started up the circular staircase. Norm gave his brother and sister a shrug and followed.

"Norm. I am worried about the site going down tonight."

"There will be no problems. Really. I promise."

"I want to be sure. I want you to do a back up now and I want you to be here at midnight so you can fix anything that goes wrong."

"My brother and sister are leaving on Sunday, and today I am showing them..."

Milena stared at Norm until he stopped talking.

"You like your job?"

"Yes."

"That's what I thought." Milena picked up her phone and started punching in numbers.

Norm slowly headed down the metal stairs to tell his brother and sister that their San Francisco tour was being postponed.

December 31, 1999

Linux Guy Rescues Microsoft by Paying $35 Internet Bill

FAIRMONT

Friday * December 31, 1999
10:03 PM

VODKA TONIC #1

Holly stood at the window and stared at the view of San Francisco spread beneath her. It looked like the last couple of hours of 1999 would sparkle into the new millennium with no problem. She turned to watch the people partying around her. Another amazing view. Expensive clothing. Exotic jewelry. Beautiful hair.

WAITER IN TUX: Can I get you a drink ma'am?

HOLLY: What do you have?

WAITER IN TUX: Everything.

HOLLY: Vodka Tonic.

VODKA TONIC #2

PHIL: You're made it.

HOLLY: I said I'd come. Here I am.

PHIL: Any trouble getting in?

HOLLY: First name on the list.

PHIL: My parents are over in the corner with the Russian and Swedish Ambassadors. I'll drag 'em over here when they are done talking politics.

HOLLY: I am ready to charm 'em whenever you want to drag 'em over.

PHIL: Want me to refresh your drink?

HOLLY: Sure.

FARNIETE (1994)

MARGARET (MOM): Phil says you almost went to Bangalore with him.

HOLLY: Almost. I didn't want to desert my fellow dot com workers on such short notice.

MARGARET: Our Phil is an impulsive boy.

CHESTER (DAD): You work at a dot com?

HOLLY: Splurch.com.

CHESTER: I've never heard of them. Have you heard of Splurch.com Margaret?

MARGARET: It rings a bell, but...

HOLLY: You'll hear about us. We're doing billboards.

MARGARET: Tasteful ones I hope.

PHIL: Holly won't have any say over what's in the billboards. A public relations firm usually comes up with the designs.

MARGARET: That's too bad. So many of those dot com billboards are in such poor taste.

CHESTER: Most of 'em don't make any sense.

PHIL: Give her a break on the billboards guys.

HOLLY: It's okay. Maybe I'll have enough courage to throw my two cents into the ring when the billboard decision passes Milena's desk.

CHESTER: Does your company have anything to do with Phil's?

HOLLY: No.

PHIL: I'm going to talk to Milena Peterson, the Splurch.com CEO. There might be some kind of strategic alliance in the future.

MARGARET: We're so glad Phil invited you to the party Holly.

HOLLY: Glad to be here. Glad to be anywhere.

MARGARET: You have to try some of this delightful wine we just opened. Chester would you pour this dear girl a glass.

CAYMUS SPECIAL SELECTION (1990)

BILL (COUSIN): Everybody was waiting for that plane to come back. I mean EVERYBODY. Finally it comes roaring over the trees and lands on the lake. It pulls up to the dock and everybody is cheering and laughing. So guess who comes walking off the plane?

HOLLY: Phil.

BILL: Right. My mom is going crazy 'cause she thought it was going to be...

HOLLY: You.

BILL: Right. Holly you are a sharp gal.

HOLLY: Sharp as a tack.

BILL: Phil walks over and hugs my mom and then his mom and then I come out from behind the palm tree and we just started having the greatest reunion party. We partied "til dawn.

HOLLY: Sounds fun.

BILL: Next time we go to the island, you have to come.

HOLLY: I have to be invited first.

BILL: I'll make sure you're invited.

HOLLY: Great.

BILL: This bottle is history. Shall we open another?

HOLLY: Why not.

THE BALVENIE CASK SCOTCH (1966)

CAROL (AUNT): Turn it UP! It's got to be real loud if I am going to start dancin' with all of you.

BUD (UNCLE): TURN IT UP! TURN IT UP!

CHUCK (BROTHER): Mr. Tuxedo! Another round of scotch for all the dancers.

WAITER IN TUX: Coming right up.

PHIL: Want to dance Holly?

HOLLY: What are you talking about? I'm already dancing. I've been dancing for the last twenty minutes. Where have you been? Start wiggling your butt and see if you can catch up with me.

PHIL: I'm wiggling my butt.

MARGARET: BYE EVERYBODY!

PHIL: BYE MOM. BYE DAD.

CHESTER: HAPPY NEW MILLENIUM!

ALL: HAPPY NEW MILLENIUM!

PORFIDIO REPOSADO TEQUILA

HOLLY: I loveth Tequila.

PHIL: Are you sure.

HOLLY: I am surrree. Give me another shot.

CHUCK: I'm in.

CAROL: Me too.

BUD: Me three.

H-2-O

HOLLY: Whersh is everybody?

PHIL: Gone home. Party's over.

HOLLY: Jusxth us.

PHIL: Yep.

HOLLY: I need a drink of wather.

PHIL: Here you go.

HOLLY: Thanths.

PHIL: You have beautiful eyes.

HOLLY: Yesth I do.

PHIL: And beautiful breasts.

HOLLY: Wat?

Y2K

Friday * December 31, 1999
11:18 PM

Milena drove past the intersection of O'Farrell and Powell - the epicenter of last year's New Year's Eve riot.

Most of the retail outlets had their windows covered by large pieces
of plywood. SFPD officers were everywhere. Revelers were cruising
the streets preparing to greet the new millennium - but not very many.
Milena counted. The celebrants out numbered the police - but not
by much.

A parade of cars swept down Powell and stopped in front of a
gleaming silver mime that was performing on the sidewalk on the
edge of Union Square. Reverend Cecil B. Williams, the head honcho
at Glide Memorial Church, stepped out of the first car. He was
scheduled to lead a midnight prayer service. Twenty-five thousand
people had been expected to show up. Milena figured if a thousand made it by midnight it would be a miracle.

Milena switched the radio to KCBS. A reporter was broadcasting from
the corner of Broadway and Columbus in North Beach. It sounded
like things were even quieter there.

Milena turned north on Market. Things got more exciting. Last
minute crowds were surging towards Embarcadero Center to watch
fireworks, laser light shows, and giant videos on both sides of the
Ferry Building. A woman had climbed to the top of a traffic light and
was gyrating to the music. Another pole climber reached over and
pulled down her pants. Thousands cheered as the bare buttocked
dancer shimmied back to the ground.

Milena decided by the time she found a parking place and got back to
the Embarcadero party she would miss the countdown. She headed-
back towards her condominium on the edge of Fisherman's Wharf.
She'd have to catch the historic moment on the tube.

Milena breathed a sigh of relief as she drove. It didn't look like there were going to be any Y2K problems. Thank God. Computers had been clicking over to 12:01 in time zone after time zone and nothing had gone wrong.

Milena hit splurch.com on her cell speed dial.

"This is splurch.com - center of the web universe."

"How's it going Norm?"

"Great. I am surfing through the channels on our TV to make sure I catch the first news report when the big meltdown starts."

"Sorry I panicked Norm. I just didn't think we could afford to have the site go down again - especially if the power went out and one of our investors happened to check on the site as soon as the juice started flowing again."

"Apology accepted."

"You don't have to wait "til midnight. Go home now."

"Does Norm get a big bonus check for this evening's way beyond the call of duty effort?"

"Yes."

"When?"

"End of the month."

"It's a deal. I am outa here."

Milena frowned. Maybe I can give Norm a bonus check at the end of the month and maybe I can't.. Maybe I can give him a payroll check at the end of the month and maybe I can't.

Milena pulled into her parking garage and tried to use the relaxation techniques her energy healer had prescribed. Hard to do. Every time she focused on the image of a smooth flowing lava stream, it filled up with cartoon devils carrying dollar signs and evil question marks.

Milena rode the elevator to the top floor. What was she worrying about? She had made every splurch.com payroll so far. Tomorrow Tom was talking to his Dad about a loan to help them get them through this rough period. Everything would be okay.

splurch.com

Milena walked into her condo, put on her pajamas, and stretched out on her large four poster bed. She pointed the remote towards the huge television screen on her bedroom wall.

Y2K was not a total party wash out. New York City was still dancing in the streets three hours after the giant olive had dropped into the martini glass at Times Square and the party at the Embarcadero Center was growing by leaps and bounds. Milena decided to catch the final West Coast countdown with Dick Clark on Fox.

5 4 3 2 1...

Milena's TV went black. She looked around the room. All her lights went off. Her electrical appliances went off. Milena ran to the window and looked into the courtyard. Total black. Fire alarms were shrieking and the courtyard started filling with screaming people.

FUCK!

She shouldn't have let Norm leave splurch.com before midnight.

"April Fool! April Fool four months early."

The lights in the complex came back on as teenage jesters poured into the condo courtyard to dance and celebrate their prank.

"Millennium joke! Ha Ha Ha!"

MILLENNIUM

$

Saturday * January 1, 2000
12:07 PM

"Tommy Boy. Get down here and give your Daddy a new millennium hug."

Tom climbed from the seat of his Gulfstream IV, and gave his beaming father a bear hug.

"Technically it's not."

"Technically it's not what?"

"Technically this is not the new millennium."

"Don't start that crap with me," said John Samoley as Tom passed the aluminum chart holder to a ground crewman decked out almost as spiffy as the Love Boat Captain. "Monsignor Crenthrow explained it to me."

"You went to church this morning?" asked Tom incredulously as the two walked towards the black Dodge Viper sitting at the edge of the private Las Vegas airstrip.

"Hell no. He was playing cards with us last night."

"Monsignor Crenthrow was playing poker with you? I thought priests took vows of poverty"

"Well he ain't going to have to take any vows this week. We cleaned him out."

"I don't know what the good father said, but technically the new millennium doesn't start until January 1, 2001."

"Bullshit" John threw the car in gear, stomped on the gas, and left twenty feet of rubber on the road towards Las Vegas. "These are AD years. You know what AD means?"

115

"Anno Domini."

"Are you being stupid again?" roared John as the speedometer crept pass 80. "BC means Before Christ so AD means After Death. The minute Our Lord died they started counting and it's now twelve hours and seventeen minutes into the new millennium."

"The Monsignor told you that?"

"That's right."

Tom laughed and wondered if this ridiculous explanation was Monsignor's revenge for his poker losses.

"Glad you came down for the party Tom. It's going to be a good 'un this year."

"They're always good," said Tom as he watched the barren desert landscape flash by at over 100 miles per hour. John Samoley had been hosting his Las Vegas Gathering for thirty years. In the beginning the event had been all business. John flew his major suppliers, vendors, and top sales people into Vegas on New Year's Day. He gave them aspirin and a hundred dollar poker chip as soon as they stepped off the plane. He provided luxury suites and twenty four hours of food, drink, and female companionship. From the first year, the party had been a roaring success. Many times, John claimed that THE GATHER-ING was the main reason he had been so successful in business for so all these years.

The event was now less a promotional event and more a get together of retired friends.

"Everybody coming this year?" asked Tom.

"Everybody that's important." John pushed the gas pedal down and the speedometer crept past 120.

"Don't you think you ought to slow down a little?"

"What are you talking about? I am in perfect health. I don't need to slow down."

"I was talking about your car speed."

"There is no speed limit posted on this Nevada highway and I need to burn out the carbon from the cylinders after all that idling waiting for you to get here." John pushed the pedal to the floor and the cacti flew by even faster. "Any news on your divorce settlement?"

"Got the ruling last week."

"You get fucked?"

"Totally."

John laughed and pounded on the steering wheel. "They get you coming and going don't they? We all want that nooky so bad. We buy 'em dinners and diamonds to get 'em in the sack. We marry 'em so we can get it regularly, and then BAM! They turn off the nooky, divorce us, and walk away with all our dough."

Tom didn't want to pursue the topic any farther. He didn't think women and divorce were so simple but John Samoley had been married and divorced five times and was pretty bitter about the subject.

"You need cash?"

Tom went rigid. Somehow his Dad could always tell when he was having financial problems. He could smell it. Tom had been planning to ask for help with splurch.com. Maybe a small loan to ease the cash flow trauma until he could pry more money out of the Board of Directors.

"Speak up BOY! Ya need money?"

Asking his Dad for money wasn't worth it. He could get through the intense grilling about splurch.com finances but the endless jokes about his inability to handle cash would be too much to bear.

"Cat got your tongue?"

"I'm okay."

"You sure?"

LAST CHANCE TOM!

"Yeah. I'm sure."

EVERQUEST

Monday * January 3, 2000
11:17 AM

Sal turned on his computer.

The smiling Mac Man flashed hello and the tube started filling with gray goop as application icons popped on at the bottom of his screen.

Sal was bored, bored, bored.

Not seeing that fucking Muni bus had been sooooooo stupid. One little moment of inattention and Sal went from THE MAN at splurch.com to A WORTHLESS PIECE OF CRUD. It was the second day of the new millennium and every other computer jockey in the Bay Area was South of Market working to build the future and he was sitting in his tiny inner sunset apartment accomplishing zero.

No... he was accomplishing less than zero.

It was two and a half weeks since the accident. An accident that Sal could have avoided by paying even the least bit of attention. He was doing everything the doctors recommended - drinking gallons of milk and getting too much sleep. His blood stream was filled with calcium and his bones were getting ample time to heal without interruption. But even if his bones were healing at lighting speed - it would be a month before the casts would be removed.

He was not sure he would be able to survive the boredom that long.

Sal's flight from bike seat to sidewalk had resulted in a horrible broken bone combination. The compound ankle fracture and split knee cap had reduced his mobility to almost zero and the broken clavicle, femur, wrist, and four bones in his right hand had cut his keyboard wizardry off at the pass. This morning, he had woken four times and been only able to force himself back to sleep three. He had turned on the television and switched through a repeat of the MTV's live New Year's Eve broadcast, a half hour ESPN bowl game highlight show, a CNN Y2K report, a DISCOVERY program featuring badly animated dinosaurs, and a weird comedy about cars racing through the Louisiana swamps on the USA Network. He finally stopped at the Sci-Fi Channel and watched the last twenty minutes of Stanley Kubrick's 2001.

Sal called splurch.com to chat with Holly but she wasn't in (Damn!). He talked to Norm for a few minutes, but Splurch wasn't experiencing any major engineering traumas, so they didn't have much to talk about. He asked Norm to transfer him to Milena so he could discuss his health insurance problem. Norm said that it was probably not a good time to talk about money because Milena was in one of her "reduce costs" modes.

He dialed up his ISP and thought about going to Yahoo for a game of chess.

Sal was a pretty good chess player, but a year ago he had played his first on-line game and his perception of his chess prowess had been violently altered. The other player was from Sydney, Australia and had cleaned his clock. Sal discovered that anytime he wanted to play - day or night - thousands of players were on Yahoo ready and willing to play. A large portion of the on-line chess players were better than him. After over 400 on-line games, Sal knew exactly how good a chess player he was. If he played someone 100 points lower than his rating, he usually won. If he played someone 100 points higher - he usually lost. If he played someone with a similar rating, it was a struggle to the last pawn. It still amazed Sal that he could be playing at 11 PM and his opponent would send him an instant message saying that he was watching the sun come up in Moscow. He was playing an intense chess game - with no time lag between the moves - against an opponent on the other side of the world.

Sal decided to try something new.

Two days ago, Mart had called to cheer him up.

"Sounds like you got some time on your hands?"

"That's right."

"Try EverQuest"

"What's that?"

"A role playing game. Some people call it EverCrack."

splurch.com

"Evercrack?"

"It's real addictive."

Sal decided to try it.

One hour later, he was creating a Wood Elf Druid.

Two hours later, his Wood Elf was foraging in the Newbie Zone outside the gates of Felwith killing low level creatures and gathering pelts.

Four hours later, he was waiting with a group of players for a monster to spawn so they could kill it and take it's loot.

Twelve hours later, he was in Everfrost defeating a Sand Giant with a Boom Spell.

Sixteen hours later, Sal was still playing.

January 2, 2000

Catering to High-tech Travelers

MAGIC

Tuesday * January 4, 2000
11:46 PM

FADE UP

<u>Interior - Night</u>

The DRAGON WELL in San Francisco Marina District.

HOLLY CHEN is sitting at a small table with
CLAIRE HELLER, her USF sophomore roommate,
and.SANDY UNGLER, an actress friend who has just
performed a small role in Tom Sethard's "Buried
Crisis" at the Magic Theater. The room is
filled with THEATER PEOPLE.

Sandy: You have to go.

Holly: I don't have to do anything.

Claire: You really have to go. You can't turn this
kind of opportunity down.

Holly: I don't really know him.

Claire: He's a millionaire... what else is there
to know?

Sandy: Go for it.

Seller (VO): Holly Chen! YOU GO FOR IT GAL!

SELLER RUMBO, another USF graduate in dreadlocks
and wearing a tattered green leather jacket hanging
to his knees appears.

Seller: Before I find out what Holly's going for,
I want to let Sandy know that she was SENSATIONAL
tonight. Give me lips.

Seller grabs Sandy's face and kisses her.

Sandy: Thank you Seller.

Claire: You really were good tonight Sandy.

Sandy: It's hard to screw up ten lines.

Holly: You're understudying the lead, right?

Sandy: Yeah. But that woman will never get sick.

Seller(chuckling wickedly): Oh...we have ways.

Claire: Hey Seller, guess what?

Seller: What?

Sandy: Phil invited Holly to go to Europe with him.

Seller sinks to his knees on the floor next to Holly.

Seller: Phil Steinberg?

Holly: Yes.

Seller: The boy zillionaire?

Holly: Yes.

Seller: Asked you to go to Europe with him?

Holly: Yes.

Seller: And you might not go?

Holly: Yes.

Seller leaps to his feet and screams.

Seller: MEDIC. WE NEED A MEDIC. A bad case of insanity at this table. MEDIC!

<u>CUT TO:</u>

Same table two hours later. The room is nearly empty.

122

Claire: When you woke up he wasn't there?

Holly: That's right. Just me - all by my lonesome.

Sandy: That's weird.

Holly: My feelings exactly. I had been dreaming about an insane scientist boring a hole into my brain. The pain was so intense it woke me up. I opened my eyes and was laying in a bed in a luxury suite at the Fairmont Hotel. All alone.

Claire: Dressed?

Holly: Under the covers and totally naked.

Claire: So...did anything happen?

Holly: I DON'T KNOW!!!! Damn. I don't think so. But I don't know. My memory of the last two party hours is non-existent.

Sandy: He just woke up and took off?

Holly: He left a note.

Holly reaches into her purse and removes the note. It is on Fairmont stationary and has obviously been folded and unfolded many times.

Holly: Here it is.

The camera zooms into the note.

Claire (READING): Holly. I got called to an emergency morning meeting and decided I shouldn't wake you. I am leaving for a four week European trip in a couple of days. Want to go? It should be lots of fun. Call me on my cell when you wake.

L.

Phil

A JOVIAL BARTENDER starts removing empty glasses from the table.

splurch.com

Bartender: Time to drink up gals.

Claire: Did you call him?

Holly: Are you kidding. I got the hell out of
there. It was too fucking weird.

Interior - Night

INTERROGATION ROOM. Holly is in handcuffs sitting
on hard back chair. A bright white light is shin-
ning in her face.

Phil (VO): Why didn't you call Phil when you
woke?

Holly doesn't speak.

Phil (VO): Why aren't you returning Phil's phone
calls?

Holly doesn't speak.

Phil (VO): Traveling through Europe together would
have been fun.

Holly doesn't speak.

Phil (VO): Come on Holly. Talk to Phil.

Holly: I want to ask you something.

Phil (VO): Sure.

Holly: What does "L" mean?

Phil doesn't respond.

Exterior - Night

TWIN PEAKS. Holly is in a flowing white gown. The
city of San Francisco sparkles behind her. Young
dot commers frantically rush past her carrying
file folders, deal memos, keyboards, computer
monitors, coffee cups, floppy disks, cell phones,
and stock options.

Opening chords of Scott McKenzie's "San Francisco (Wear Some Flowers In Your Hair)."

Holly smiles and sings.

Holly:

> *Am I flying from San Francisco?*
> *Should I carry some condoms in my purse*
> *If I am flying from San Francisco,*
> *Will I be traveling with a total jerk*

FADE TO BLACK

Too much fantasy or not enough, wondered Holly as she named the file MAGIC and moved it into her FILM folder.

January 5, 2000

Individual Investors Gaining Status

ONE MORE EVENT

Thursday * January 6, 2000
3:18 PM

Norm pounded his keyboard and spun around to face Holly.

"THAT'S ONE MORE EVENT."

He strained to get his frustration under control.

"Tell Milena that I can't do it right now."

"I will," Holly said. "But she's not going to like it."

"It's not that I WON'T do it, I CAN'T do it right now. We're having a meltdown and her request is just one more event. One more event more than I can handle at this point in time."

"I'll try to explain that."

Norm rubbed his temples and said softly. "I am sorry Holly. I didn't mean to yell at you. We need more help. We need to hire another engineer. At least until Sal gets back."

"Don't worry about it Norm," said Holly as she grabbed one of Norm's hands and kissed it. "I don't take your frustration explosions personally. If I did, I would have been out the door a long time ago."

"Great," said Norm as he spun back to face the crisis exploding on his computer screen.

Ten minutes later Holly was back at the door of Norm's cubicle.

"Milena would like you to come up to her loft before you leave tonight.'

"Is she mad?"

"Hard to tell."

"Okay. Tell her I'll be there."

126

Norm spent the rest of the afternoon planning how to explain to Milena why he couldn't drop everything whenever she asked him to do something. He finished most of his work by 4:30 but found some extra projects to work on so he wouldn't be climbing to Milena's command center too early.

At 6:30, he finally scaled the red metal circular stairs to face the music. As as his head popped above the wooden deck, Milena waved.

"Hey Norm."

"Hey Milena."

Milena held up a glass of wine.

"Join me?"

"It's a long haul back to San Jose, but I guess one glass won't hurt. I am sorry. We were having major problems today."

Milena cut him off. "Everything okay now?"

"Yeah but..."

"Look at this."

Milena held up a copy of Upside Magazine.

"Look at what?"

Milena pointed to an article on JDS Uniphase.

"JDS makes fiber optic stuff."

"That's right The price of their stock went from $12 to $242. That means every share of stock gained $230. If someone held a thousand shares of stock of that company they've made two hundred and thirty thousand dollars."

"Wow. Almost a quarter of a million dollars."

"You have more splurch.com stock options than any other employee."

"If you say so."

"The day we go public you are going to be worth a lot of money."

'I'll be in lock up. I won't be able to cash in for awhile."

splurch.com

"What we're doing here is working to make sure that splurch.com has a successful IPO so we can all make a lot of money."

Milena took a sip of her wine. Norm had no idea where she was going with this.

"We are a team and we all have the same goal. But reaching that goal is not easy. It's requires a lot of effort on all our parts."

"You can count on me," said Norm.

"Good, because I need your help. We are having a cash flow problem."

Norm set his glass down.

"We have a number of investors who put money into splurch.com every month."

"They didn't just give us a big check at the beginning?"

"They did that but they also committed to putting money into our account every month as long as we hit our milestones. When the site went down a couple of weeks ago, some of the investors decided they wouldn't put anymore money into splurch.com until we got our act together."

"Didn't they sign a contract?"

"They did."

"So we sue them if they don't give us money."

"And we'd win - five years from now - when splurch.com is a faint memory."

"That sucks."

"We need your help Norm. I am hoping that you would be willing to take a pay cut for a couple of pay periods."

A shudder went through Norm.

"This is probably just crying wolf. Tom went to Las Vegas to ask his dad for a loan to tide us over, but I wanted to talk to you and some of the other key employees so we'd be prepared for the worse."

"How much of a cut."

"50%."

Norm stared at his wine glass and tried to quell the waves of panic attacking his central nervous system.

January 6, 2000

Dow Up 125

ASPEN

Friday * January 7, 2000
10:18 AM

"What do you do?"

"Move cash around," Tom said as he turned and smiled at the delightful Ski Bunny riding on the chair beside him.

"Let me guess," said Bunny. "Bank teller?"

"Ahhhh...right...sort of a bank teller," said Tom as they approached the end of their climb together.

"I am new at this. I might have trouble getting off," Bunny said raising the safety bar.

Tom groaned. He hated riding chair lifts with beginners. There were always problems. This was no exception. As soon as Bunny tried to stand up, she fell into Tom. Tom tried to focus on the contact he was making with this gorgeous creature, but when both his skis popped off at the end of the tumble, he couldn't control his anger.

"Stay in the beginner's area until you learn to ski," he barked.

"I am sorry."

"Don't be sorry. Just stay off this lift."

Tom angrily removed snow from the bottom of his boots, slipped back into his bindings, and pushed off towards the runs.

Another gorgeous Rocky Mountain day. The sun was hot, the packed powder was sparkling, and the blue sky was filled with fluffy clouds slowly making their way from horizon to horizon.

Tom headed down Sunrise, the Blue Square intermediate run he had just skied. A couple of years ago, he would have switched to Cliff Hanger, a Black Diamond expert run, but, at this point in his life, he was not interested in testing himself - just in blasting full speed down the mountain.

Tom attacked.

Knees together. Watch that snowboarder. Those slow skiers are stopping - get to the right. Skis together. Okay. That woman is turning this way...ahhhhh...missed her...watch those kids...watch 'em...skis together...too fast...turn turn...ice...turn....slip.. turn...skis together. Bump...bump...too fast...caught an edge....get control...get control. Slow down...turn...stop...breathe.

Tom stopped and gasped for air a quarter of the way down the mountain. A couple of years ago, he would have made it all the way to the bottom without stopping. Well...maybe most of the way down without stopping.

Tom approached the broad white expanse at the end of the run. He aimed towards the "ski corral" in front of the main lodge instead of the lift line. As he took the wooden token he'd gotten in exchange for his skis and poles, he glanced at the man with the wrap around sunglasses behind him.

"Staner Lipton?"

"That's me," said Staner holding out his gloved hand. "John Samoley?"

"Tom Samoley," said Tom as their gloves joined. "John is my father."

"Sorry. I always do that. Mix up fathers and sons."

"No problem."

"I guess I met your father before I met you."

"You came to one of his Vegas parties a couple years ago."

"Hundred dollar poker chips when you get off the plane."

"Right."

"Fun."

"Can I buy you lunch?" asked Tom.

"Sure," said Staner as they the two men clomped up the metal lodge stairs. "How's life at splurch.com?"

"Fine" said Tom as they both studied the rows of food and drink in the refrigerators lining the back wall.

"Can't wait until that splurch.com IPO. I want to rake in some of those instant bucks like everybody else."

"We are having a little cash flow problem right now," said Tom cautiously. "A couple of our Board members got cold feet. They haven't deposited their monthly contributions."

"Why?"

"Panicked about the site going down."

"It's the computer biz. Computers break. What did they expect when they invested in a dot com," laughed Staner as he grabbed three Red Bulls. "You want to win the race - you have to be prepared for bumps in the road."

"Would you tell 'em that?" laughed Tom.

"Even better," replied Staner, "I'll cover their contributions. We can't let a couple of chicken investors slow down our trip to the splurch.com promise land."

"Great," said Tom.

The gal at the register held up Tom's card. "This card was rejected."

"It's good."

"It doesn't say why it was rejected."

"Probably the magnetism," said Tom as he grabbed a plastic bag off the counter, wrapped his card in it, and handed it back. "Try this."

The register gal looked at the card in the bag skeptically.

"Try it."

She ran the card wrapped in the plastic bag through the machine.

Accepted.

"Wow," said Staner. "Great trick."

"When it comes to money," said Tom. "I got a million of 'em."

BILLBOARDS

Wednesday * January 12, 2000
9:37 AM

"How much?

"Twenty-five thousand dollars."

"Twenty-five thousand dollars for one billboard?"

"Yes."

"For one month?"

"Yes."

Milena turned to Holly. "Do you have the rate card?"

Holly opened the bulging promotional folder in front of her and searched until she found the Canston & Noble rate card. She past it to Milena who looked at it and then passed it to Jason Curley, the senior account rep for splurch.com's new public relations firm. Jason glanced at it and smiled at Milena.

"The rate card is four months old. This is the new economy - things change quickly."

"Sure," smiled Milena back. "But nobody raises their prices three hundred percent in four months."

"True," continued the confident silver haired salesman on the far side of the gleaming brass table. "But this is a generic rate card for normal billboard placement. You want a billboard on Highway 101. That's a prime location. The whole industry will see it. You also want it in place by March. That's a rush order."

Milena took a sip of her coffee and thought about what to do. Tom had called Friday night with wonderful news. Not only had Staner Lipton committed to covering the impending splurch.com cash crunch, but Tom had then used Staner's generosity to strong arm the other reluctant investors into coughing up their monthly subscription contributions. They were back on solid financial ground.

The road to an IPO was now wide open. Dreams of instant riches and life-long security were again lulling Milena to eight hours of uninterrupted sleep a night - sleep that she had sorely been missing during the previous month of chaos and crisis.

Milena thought about the splurch.com roadshow she and Tom were embarking on in mid-April. Together they would visit bankers and investment groups around the country to explain what a fantastic investment splurch.com was. Before they started the tour, however, they had to make sure that everyone knew about the company and they had to dramatically increase the number of eyeballs visiting the site each day. They had to create massive brand awareness. Even more important, they had to create investment banker awareness and Silicon Valley tech awareness. They had to convince the web biz high rollers that splurch.com was a winner.

"Let's talk radio," said Milena.

"Sure," said Jason as he pulled out some dramatic four-color Canston & Noble radio brochures. "The challenge with radio is the large number of stations in each market. It's easy to target and hit a specific demographic but almost impossible to hit a general audience without buying a broad range of different kinds of radio stations."

"I want to just buy a bunch of spots on KNBR next month."

"That's the other challenge," said Jason. "Almost every radio station in the major tech centers, like the Bay Area, is sold out for the first quarter of this year. We might be able to work something out with KNBR - but it will be costly."

"What about magazines?"

"I am afraid we couldn't get into any of the major national periodicals until May," said Jason. "We could probably do something in USA Today.

"USA Today!" laughed Holly. "Who reads that?"

Jason frowned at Holly, "A lot of Americans read USA Today."

"Americans that don't have computers," muttered Holly under her breath.

"I think the billboard on Highway I01 and maybe some wild television spots on FOX will get us started," said Milena. "You've talked to the MTV people about producing the television commercial for us?"

"They're waiting for your call."

"Great." Milena pulled a large sheet of artwork from her briefcase and placed it on the table. "This is the design I want to use for the billboard. It was done by a fabulous artist friend of mine - Addrianne Lister. She also designed the logo we are using on the site."

Jason stared at the multi-media art work laying on the table in front of him. "Unique," he finally said.

"That's right," said Milena as she stroked the cat hair that marked the borders of the design. "This will cut through all the clutter."

No one said anything for almost a minute and finally Holly gulped, "What's the message?"

"Simple," said Milena. "Splurch.com is different."

January 13, 2000

SF Linux Vendor To Get
$57 Million Infusion

WHY ME?

Saturday * January 15, 2000
4:25 AM

Sal furiously pedaled down the twisting mountain road. He was going to win. No one else was even close.

Brannnnnng.

The blacktop was smooth and fast. He was moving like the wind. Like an engine. Like a God.

Brannnnnng

NOISE? Something was wrong. Tire! It was the front tire. He was weaving.

Brannnnnng.

Losing control. Heading for the guard rail. The cliff.

What was that NOISE!

Brann...Clink.

Sal opened his eyes and focused on the plastic alarm clock he had just silenced. 4:25. Why would he set his alarm for 4:25 in the morning?

EVERQUEST!

Right. He was meeting his two traveling companions at the gates of Felwith at 5 am.

For the last week, Sal's Wood Elf Druid had been journeying through virtual worlds with a Barbarian Warrior and a Dwarf Cleric. The three characters formed a classic traveling trio: a fighter to lead through unexplored territory, a magician to conjure up spells to defeat the creatures that attacked along the way, and a healer to restore health after the violent confrontations.

Sal struggled to sit up, and then struggled to stand next to the bed on his one good foot. He hopped to the bathroom, and leaned on the wall to urinate. He then bounced towards the kitchen. As soon as he reached the red plastic chair in front of the coffee maker, he collapsed. Living without the right side of his body was getting old. It had been six weeks since his bike accident. The horrible itching had finally gone away but the frustration of being unable to do anything physical had become unbearable.

The casts were coming off in two weeks. Hallelujah!

Every cloud has a silver lining Sal thought as he watched the coffee drip. Without the accident, he would never have started playing Everquest and wouldn't have met his two new virtual friends. He laughed about their decision to stop play and resume their adventure at this ungodly hour of the morning.

Last night their server had been loaded to the max and over two thousand people were traveling through Felwith. Another MOB had just come pouring through and knocked them off their pursuit of a Gargon. Gersta (Barbarian Warrior) suggested they stop and talk strategy. Felix (Dwarf Cleric) and Swoop (Sal's Wood Elf Druid) agreed.

Gersta: Too many lower levels running around.

Felix: Amateur hour.

Gersta: Let's nap and come back in six hours.

Swoop: 5 am?

Felix: Less crowded.

Gersta: More fun.

Felix: K

Gersta: Cradorth Gate.

Swoop: K

Flex: K

Sal hopped to his computer carrying his no spill coffee cup. He looked at the clock. Time to load in a couple more automatics. Since Sal only had a left hand and one right finger to work with, he had major problems communicating with his keyboard. Many times he was torturously trying to type a response when the other players decided he was ignoring them and took off. He finally figured out a way to program his computer so that an entire phrase appeared in the dialogue box when he hit the command button and one, two, or three additional keys.

Command/N = Let's head North.

Command/NF = Let's head North fast.

Command/NFR = Let's head North fast and regroup.

The caffeine elevated his blood sugar, and Sal thought about his future. It looked rosy. Tom Samoley - the man himself - had called yesterday.

"Back in two weeks," said Tom.

"Yep."

"We miss ya. The IPO is the first week of April and the site has to be rolling 24-7 until then."

"You can count on me."

"Great."

"Can I ask you about something, Tom?."

"Sure. Sal you can ask me about anything."

"The health insurance company still hasn't agreed to cover my bills."

"I wouldn't know about that. That's Milena's area. See you in two weeks."

Click.

Oh well. Once he got back to work, he was sure his health insurance trauma would get worked out.

The phone rang.

Had to be Gersta making sure he was up and ready to play. The Everquest partners had exchanged real life phone numbers a few weeks ago. That's when Sal discovered Felix was actually a forty year old banker living in Portland Oregon and Gersta was a twenty six year old, extremely pleasant and very bright, female programmer living in San Mateo.

"Swoop ready to roll," he barked into the phone.

"I must have the wrong number. I was trying to call Sal Zaldivar."

"Holly?

"Sal?

"That's me."

"Who's Swoop?"

"Long story. What's up?"

"Sorry it's the middle of the night. I had to talk to somebody."

"No problem."

"Phil Steinberg just called from Bulgaria."

"Expensive call."

"He asked me to marry him."

January 16, 2000

Vast Supply of Dollars
Leads to Flood of Deals

CREATIVE

$

Wednesday * January 19, 2000
10:17 AM

Tom gunned his Ferrari through the stop light at Van Ness and Mission.

No cops. No problem.

Two creatives from MTV had flown in from New York City the night before. They were staying at the Milano Hotel and Milena had scheduled a meeting for ten this morning.

Tom told Milena that whatever she wanted to do with the television spot was fine with him.

"Are you sure?" she asked.

"You're the marketing genius. I am just the guy that makes sure the cash gets to the bank."

"You should come to the first creative session."

"Nope. This is your baby, Milena."

Last night Tom had been watching "Nash Bridges" and was suddenly flooded with terrific ideas for the splurch.com commercial. He almost called Milena to discuss them with her, but then decided to just show up at the meeting and share his ideas with everybody.

On the drive up from Woodside, Tom started thinking about the kind of effect the television spots would have when splurch.com hit the market. If the commercial was an out of the box creative winner - like the Pets.com sock puppet spots - it would produce rivers of free ink and the first day price would shoot up to the moon.

Tom pulled into the Milano driveway, threw the keys to the attendant, and headed into the lobby. On the elevator ride to the top floor, he decided the television commercial was far more important that he first thought, and something he'd better keep a careful eye on.

"Tom," said Milena as he strode into the room. She put down the story board she was holding. "What are you doing here?"

"Didn't want to miss the fun."

Tom extended his hand to the paisley shirted man with the goatee and Pork Pie hat sitting on the couch next to Milena. "Tom Samoley."

"John Buyson."

"What's your role on this project, John?"

"Writer producer."

"Great."

Tom extended his hand to the long haired woman in the skin tight black leather outfit standing behind the couch. "Tom Samoley."

"Cinda Senson. Director."

"Glad to meet ya Cinda."

An awkward pause settled over the room.

Tom stretched out on the chair by the couch. "Have I missed much?"

Cinda and Burt were just taking me through the ideas they have story boarded for us."

"Can you catch me up?"

"Sure," Milena said. "This first spot opens with a cornucopia that..."

"A what?"

"Cornucopia. A shell like vessel that..."

"Let me look."

John turned the boards toward Tom.

"Too old fashion. People see something like that and they won't know what you're talking about."

Another awkward pause.

"What's the next idea?"

splurch.com

John put the first set of boards at the bottom of the pile and Cinda leaned over and said, "This spot starts with a couple in a park. They are in love. They're talking about..."

Tom cut her off. "We need to grab 'em. If we start with something people don't understand like the corna-whatever or a scene they've seen a million times like a loving couple in a park - we lose."

No one said anything.

"Do you mind if I just cruise through the boards on my own?"

"Sure," said John.

Tom sat on the couch and started flipping through the boards. When he got through all seven presentations, he tapped on the pile and said, "Great work. These ideas will work for old economy clients, but we need something new and different for splurch.com - something that sets us apart from all the other dot coms."

John, Cinda, and Milena nodded their heads in agreement, as Tom leaped off the couch and started pacing around the room.

"Let me run three words by you. Explosions and Don Johnson."

"What are you talking about Tom?" asked Milena quietly.

Tom raised one finger. "The explosions wake 'em up." He raised his second finger. "Don Johnson delivers our message."

"Don Johnson?" asked Cinda.

"Total believable guy."

"Also very expensive," said John.

"Doesn't matter," said Tom. "This splurch.com spot is too important to let money get in the way of it being the best it can be."

"Maybe we should put some soldiers in the spot," said Cinda.

"And a couple of car crashes," added John.

Tom looked at the two giggling MTV veterans. "Great ideas. Let's make them happen."

DMV

Friday * January 21, 2000
3:18 PM

Twenty eight people.

Norm counted again.

Seven and eight might be together. Hard to tell. Norm decided to count them separately so if they approached the DMV window together he would have something to be happy about.

The man in the polo shirt was leaving the window. Alright. Twenty seven people to go. No. Polo shirt was just reaching into his tote bag. Still twenty eight. Dang.

Three nineteen. Norm figured he would get to the window in about an hour. It had been a stupid mistake not to call and make an appointment. The people in the appointment line were taking less then ten minutes. But phone appointments had to be made two weeks in advance and Norm's registration was expiring in two days.

Norm took out his cell and hit speed dial for his sister in Boston. His new calling plan offered a week of unlimited calls anywhere in the United States. 6:30 PM. on the East Coast. With any luck his sister would be home starting dinner.

Opening drums of the Bohemian Love Song

This is Sarah Dotoshay. This is my machine. This is your chance to leave a message of any length.

Music builds

Herrrrrre it comes...

Music builds

It's commmmmmming...

143

splurch.com

Music full

It's here... the... BEEP

"This is Norm. I am waiting in a DMV line. Things at splurch.com are going great. The pay cut trauma is over and the IPO is back on track. Old Norm is keeping the servers cooking and the web site available to the world. I am also scoping out places for desks for you and Chris when those IPO bucks start pouring in and Milena is desperate to hire more good people. Try ya later."

A middle aged black man standing in front of Norm turned around.

"Could I make a local call on your cell phone?"

"Sure," said Norm.

"I left mine in the cab. My daughter is expecting me in fifteen minutes and I don't want to lose my place looking for a pay phone."

"No problem," said Norm as he handed the cell to the pleasant man in the three piece suit.

When the man finished his call he handed the cell phone back to Norm. "You work for a dot com?"

"Yep."

"Be careful. I don't think it's going to last."

"What isn't going to last?"

"That dot com stuff. You have to make money to stay in business."

"You're probably right."

"I'd quit now and get a real job."

"I've got too many stock options to walk away now," laughed Norm.

"You're going to be sorry.

Norm looked at the line in front of him. Twenty three people. He had plenty of time to deliver a speech on the new economy.

"Do you know how many people go on-line every day?" he asked.

"No idea."

"Ten thousand. That means every day there are ten thousand new customers and everybody knows that business is based on three things - location, location, and location. So what's a better location - the corner of main and central or the desk in somebody's den?"

"You have to make money to stay in business."

"We'll make money. In the long run, we'll make a lot of money."

"For your sake - I hope so."

The topic switched to the adventures of Mayor Willie Brown. Norm and his new friend talked non-stop until their shot at the window.

After Norm paid his registration the clerk said, "Did you know your driver's license is expired?"

"What?"

"You were mailed a renewal form a couple of months ago."

"I knew I was missing some mail." Norm slapped his thigh. "I remember. It's in the backyard next to the satellite dish. The wind had disconnected the cable and when I went out to fix it that day, I put down the mail. It's probably still sitting there."

"Better get it renewed."

"Let's do it now."

"Can't do it at this window. You have to wait in that line," the clerk said pointing to a line stretching out the door. "Or make an appointment."

Norm decided he would deal with the license later, and ran to his car. It was 4:30. He promised Milena he would be back at splurch.com before five. If he hurried he could make it. He took a left on Harrison. There was no left turn on Harrison between 4 PM and 6 PM.

Red lights in the rear view mirror.

Damn.

"Would you hand me your license, sir?"

The officer studied the license and said, "This license has expired."

Double Damn.

145

CHA CHA CHA

Thursday * February 3, 2000
8:13 PM

"We're not getting married."

"I agree. We're not getting married."

"Great."

"Not this month. How about next month?"

"Philllllllll...!"

The harried waiter approached Holly and Phil's small table in the back of Cha Cha Cha with another plate of food.

"Very hot," he announced as he pushed aside the three previous deliveries to make room for the latest culinary delight.

"How many dishes coming?" asked Holly.

"Four."

"And then there's dessert," added Phil.

"Profiteroles with Sharffenberg chocolate sauce," announced the waiter as he saluted and headed off to deliver more dishes to tables of hungry patrons.

Holly picked up her glass of wine and took another sip. Just a sip. She wasn't going to get drunk tonight. She wasn't going to make that mistake again.

"You have to stop joking about this wedding thing," Holly said. "It's too dangerous. Gosh darn it. You could break a gal's heart with that kinda of talk."

"I am not joking," said Phil, "and I would never break your heart - ever."

"Let's review this relationship," Holly said. "How long have Holly and Phil known each other?"

"Two months and two days." Phil glanced at his watch. "Almost to the minute."

"And how much time have Holly and Phil actually spent together in those two months?"

"It's not the quantity of time together. It's the quality." Phil took both of Holly's hands in his. "The minutes we have spent together have been some of the happiest in my life."

Holly stuck her finger in her mouth and pretended to vomit.

Phil laughed. "This is why I love you. You never let me get too serious. You make every minute joyful."

Holly pretended to vomit even more violently and fell out of her chair. "Your bullshit is killing me."

The restaurant customers stared as Holly lay twitching on the floor.

"She's joking," Phil said loudly as he grabbed Holly's hand and tried to pull her up. "Really. This is just a joke."

"Stop all this marriage talk and I'll recover," said Holly through closed eyes and clenched teeth.

The other restaurant patrons were becoming concerned about the young woman groaning on the floor. Phil beamed a smile in all directions and said, "She's just being funny."

No one was buying it.

Phil leaned down and whispered, "Holly you have to get off the floor."

"No more wedding bullshit?"

"Agreed."

Holly hopped back into her chair, took a swig of wine, and ate a couple more mushrooms. "What do you think dish six will be?"

Smiles all around.

A limo appeaared when Phil and Holly walked out of the restaurant.

"A moolight drive," asked Phil as they climbed into the silver limo where a bottle of chilled Veuve Cliquot awaited.

"Sure," said Holly as she slid across the leather upholstery. "Holly Chen doesn't have to be at work tomorrow morning at 8 am. That's the other Holly Chen."

They parked at the top of Twin Peaks and finished the bottle of champagne. The entire Bay Area twinkled at their feet.

"Holly, can I talk seriously about our relationship for just a minute."

Holly grabbed his wrist and held his watch in front of her face. "Go."

"I think the reason I have been successful in business is because I make quick decisions about what works. Everything about you works for me and I am sure it will work forever."

"Thirty seconds."

"My parents and my relatives all think you are great. You were the hit of the party at the Fairmont. My cousin Bill couldn't stop talking about how much fun you were."

"Ten seconds."

"And I love you."

"Times up," said Holly as she gave Phil his wrist back. "Did you see that Mookie Blaylock went 10 for 14 against Vancouver last night?"

Phil laughed and leaned forward to whisper to the driver.

Chopin played through the six limo speakers as the limo raced down Twin Peaks, crossed the Golden Gate Bridge, and swung onto the Sausalito Boat Dock.

"I want you to meet someone," said Phil as they climbed out of the car and walked out on the dock together.

They stopped in front of a large sailboat that was glistening in the moonlight.

"Holly Chen, I want you to meet the latest member of the Steinberg family."

Phil pointed to the bow of the boat and Holly stared at the words

HOLLY DREAM in large gold letters.

"Want to go for a ride," said Phil as he stepped onto swaying deck and reached back for Holly's hand.

Holly climbed aboard and thought, what the hell am I getting myself into.

February 5, 2000

Fiber-Optic Company
Stock Rockets $136

SHOOT

Monday * February 7, 2000
4:47 PM

"FIRE IN THE HOLE."

The scream by the curly haired man in the black Metallica shirt (first assistant director) was so intense that Sal almost ducked down behind the sand bag wall.

Good thing he didn't. The series of exploding wooden crates on the edge of the abandoned San Francisco pier was really fun to watch.

As soon as the final box exploded, an assortment of men (extras) in full military combat gear (wardrobe) poured onto the dock waving fake M-16's (props) and pretending to search for something.

Five cameras were capturing the action simultaneously. The main camera, a 35 mm Panaflex Platinum, was sitting on a heavy metal cart (dolly) and slowly being pushed forward by a man in a 49er sweat shirt (grip). A woman in a Laker jacket (shooter) sat on a little round chair attached to the cart. She was watching the burning crates and frantic soldiers through a rubber eye piece (view finder) to make sure the picture was perfect (framed correctly).

Camera two was on a tall tripod capturing the flames flashing on the angry soldier's faces with a close-up lens (telephoto). The third and fourth cameras - set up on the far right and far left sides of the action - were capturing interesting angles of the soldiers in slow motion (slo-mo). The fifth camera (hand held) was being operated by Cinda Senson from a crane hovering just above the action.

Sal laughed out loud.

QUESTION: Does life get any better than this?

ANSWER: It does not.

The crew spent the entire day setting up for this early evening shot (magic hour). It was going to be the opening scene of the television commercial (spot). Sal had come into work at 5 AM so he could leave work early and watch the filming without feeling guilty. It was the first time he had climbed aboard his ten speed since his casts were removed a week ago.

QUESTION: Was being healthy the most important thing in the world?

ANSWER: It was.

Pretend soldiers continued to race around the pier as the cameras rolled. Finally Cinda put her camera down and barked "cut" into a walky-talky. Young crew members (production assistants) from locations all over the pier (shooting set) loudly repeated her command as people with fire extinguishers (special effects crew) poured onto the pier to put out the burning boxes.

Milena Peterson (splurch.com CEO) and Tom Samoley (Lead Investor and Acting Chief Financial Officer) were standing with John Buyson (producer) staring intently at the five small televisions (monitors) that were lined up on a long black folding table directly behind Sal. The tiny televisions were showing the images being captured by the five film cameras (video tap).

John (into walky talky): Looked great Cinda. Your hand held stuff rocked my world.

Cinda (from walky-talky): Felt good to me.

Tom: Should we do it again?

John: We don't need to.

Milena: That take looked great Tom.

Tom: I don't know.

John: We've got an awful lot of film in the can for only ten seconds of commercial.

Tom: I want to do it again.

First Assistant Director: We're losing light and if we do it again we're into overtime penalties for the entire crew.

Tom: Do it again.

John pulled a clipboard from his bag, filled in some numbers on the attached sheet (change order form) and held it out to Tom.

John: It's your money.

Tom: That's right.

John (into walky-talky): We're going again.

First Assistant Director: BACK TO ONE!

The production assistants echoed the 1st AD's command and the entire crew sprang into action. The special effects team carried un-exploded crates onto the set, the extras went back to their off-camera starting spots, and the main dolly was rolled back to it's original location (first position).

"Sal, guess what?"

Sal spun around. Holly was standing behind him smiling.

"What."

"Don Johnson is doing the commercial."

"How do you knowt?"

"Milena just got a call from his secretary. They are shooting a "Nash Bridges" scene in Chinatown tomorrow and Don agreed to let us shoot his line during the lunch break."

"I wish I could be there."

"Milena said we could go if we brought our lap tops."

"Why?"

"I think she wants to impress Don Johnson."

QUESTION: Would Sal be able to get Don Johnson's autograph tomorrow?

ANSWER: He was sure going to try.

EDIT

$

Friday * February 18, 2000
2:36 PM

"Splurch.com," said Don Johnson.

"What do we think?" asked the editor with the flaming pink shirt and the continuous thoughtful grin.

"Getting there," said Tom from the couch in the back of the editing room. "What do you guys think?"

Producer John Buyson immediately said, "I think we're there."

Director Cinda Senson, who was sitting beside the editor at the oak and leather console filled with knobs, dials, and flashing red, green, and yellow meters stared at Don Johnson's frozen face on the large screen in front of her. Finally she turned and said, "I think I liked it better when the cut was a few frames earlier."

"Shall we go back and look at it that way," asked the editor.

No one said anything.

Finally Tom said, "I guess."

The editor hit a series of buttons and Don Johnson was once again saying, "Splurch.com" directly at them.

"Perfect," said the director.

"Doesn't work for me," said Tom.

"Why not?" asked Cinda angrily.

"It doesn't seem natural."

"This is a commercial - there's nothing natural about it."

"Bursting bladder," announced the grinning editor. "Break time."

153

splurch.com

The MTV people headed out the door to take a smoke break in the parking lot as Tom picked up the courtesy phone on the glass table in front of his couch and called splurch.com.

"Have we done the media buy?" Tom asked as soon as Milena came on.

"Not yet."

"Double the television."

"What?"

"This commercial is going to be unbelievably great. I want to make sure we run it enough to make a real impact."

"I suppose we could buy more cable spots."

"No. I want to buy more network spots."

"Those are tough to come by."

"I don't care."

"And expensive."

"It will be worth every penny when the IPO hits the street and the splurch.com stock price sky-rockets. Every banker in the investment universe is going to realize that splurch.com is the hottest dot com investment since eBay and the coolest since Salon."

"I'll call the agency in the morning."

"Call them now."

"Okay," said Milena. "What if they ask for payment? Some of the agencies are asking for money up front because so many dot coms are demanding prime time commercial real estate."

"We'll just dip into the Staner Lipton emergency bank account."

"What are you talking about?"

"That money that Staner said he'd give us to cover the shortage we were going to have this month. He told me at Aspen he would send us a check as soon as he got back from London. Since none of our investors ended up withholding their monthly subscription contributions we should re-purpose those Lipton bucks."

"Staner's check never arrived."

"What?"

"I called his accountant to find out when they were sending it and she said Staner never told her anything about it."

"Shit," Tom screamed as he pounded his fist into the cushion. "I should sue that lying asshole."

"That would really help our public image when we go IPO."

"Try to make the media buys without any up front cash."

"If they won't do it?"

"We'll figure something out."

"Holly just finished making all the hotel, plane, and car reservations for our Road Show. Do you think the world is ready for the Tom and Milena Big Pitch?"

"Thirty cities - thirty days - can't wait," sang Tom. "All first class?"

"Of course. Nothing but the best for splurch.com. She charged it on the VISA."

"The CitiBank VISA?"

"Yeah. I think that was what she used."

"She should have used the American Express."

The editing team came pouring back into the room.

"Got to go," said Tom.

"Ohhhh...one more thing," said Milena. "South Bay Realty faxed us the lease for the new San Jose office space. The company there now has agreed to move out in May so we can move in June 1st. They want us to sign for five years with six months paid in full. Shall we do it?"

"How much per month?"

"Five dollars per square foot."

"Sign it. Got to go."

The editor stood by his chair and announced, "Maybe we should give ourselves a break from the edit and spend some time listening to the music choices."

"Great idea," said Tom.

As the pulsating beat of the first music choice filled the room, Tom leaned back and closed his eyes.

Man this dot com stuff was so great. You get to be creative and make tons of money at the same time.

A perfect business to be in.

A perfect time to be alive.

February 24, 2000

NASDAQ Jumps 168 to Record

DANCING IN THE DARK

Saturday * February 26, 2000
10:09 AM

"Sing it Bruuuuuceeeee."

You can't start a fire.

Norm danced across his living room doing a combination of the Watusi, Swim, and Twist.

You can't start a fire without a spark.

Norm's three cats were hiding under the couch staring wide eyed as their insane provider gyrated in front of them.

This gun's for hire.

Norm pretended to shoot all three cats with his pistol finger.

Even if we're just dancing in the dark.

The phone rang. Norm picked it up and clicked on the speaker phone.

"EVEN IF WE'RE JUST DANCING IN THE DARK," Norm sang along as the Springsteen refrain repeated.

"TOO LOUD," Norm's brother Chris shouted from the speaker

"I GOT THE VOLUME TO ELEVEN," Norm hollered as the song faded.

"I thought the volume control only went to ten."

"That was BST."

"BST?"

"Before Spinal Tap. You remember that joke in the movie, right?"

"Yeah."

"After I watched that movie for the fourth time, I re-designed all my volume knobs."

"As a homage?"

"Sure...whatever that is."

"It's..."

Norm cut him off, "I know what it is."

The opening chords of "Born in the USA" filled the room.

"TURN IT DOWN!" shouted Chris.

Norm reached over and spun the volume knob down. "Better?"

"Is Norm going crazy out there on the left coast?"

"My cats think so." Norm reached under the couch and picked up Seymour, his long haired tabby. "I just finished figuring out how much money I'll be worth when splurch.com goes public."

"How much?"

"Here are the numbers," said Norm as he picked up the yellow pad he had been scribbling on before his celebration dance. "Three companies went public yesterday. Granthan Textiles, Bosco Systems, and Brace.com. Granthan, which makes women's undergarments, opened at five dollars and closed at seven dollars and fifty cents. So yesterday, anyone with one hundred shares of Granthan made two hundred and fifty dollars."

"That's a lot of Big Macs, but that won't pay the rent," laughed Chris.

"Hang on! Bosco, which makes chemical testing equipment, opened at ten dollars and closed at twenty eight dollars. So everyone with one hundred stocks of Bosco made..."

"One thousand eight hundred dollars."

"And now...drum roll please...Brace.com, which aggregates construction web sites opened the day at seven dollars and closed at...are you ready for this...two hundred and fifty-two dollars and twenty five cents."

Both brothers waited and finally Norm broke the silence. "Someone with one hundred shares of Brace.com would have made twenty-four thousand five hundred and twenty five dollars...AND...good old Norm has options on TWO HUNDRED THOUSAND SHARES of splurch.com... YOU DO THE MATH!"

Norm cranked the volume back to eleven, and sang his own lyrics to the Springsteen's anthem, "FUCK YOU MONEY... HERE I COME."

"BYE NORM," Chris shouted from the speaker.

Ten minutes later the phone rang again. Norm checked caller ID. He switched off the stereo, and collapsed on the couch.

"Hi Sarah."

"Hey Norm. Chris said I'd better check up on you. He said you were going crazy out there."

"Not any more. Dancing to Bruce took too much energy out of this old man."

"He said you're going to be rich."

"That's right. On April 3rd your brother will be a very wealthy man."

"April 3rd?"

"The day splurch.com goes public."

"Isn't there some kind of waiting period before you cash in."

"A hundred and eighty days...but time flies when you're filthy rich."

"Normy - aren't you being premature with this celebration? Remember the hand held computer gizmo that was going to make you so rich?"

"If that asshole hadn't blown the marketing budget, it would have."

"The stock market is not a sure thing."

"In the last two years, every engineer I know has hit the stock option jackpot. Splurch.com is doing great. We're attracting thousands of new eyeballs every day, the national television ads start next week. They just put up a billboard on 101."

"What's on the billboard?"

"I have no idea," laughed Norm, "but you can make out the words splurch.com - which I guess is all that really counts."

"I hope you're right. Chris and I are seriously thinking about moving out there."

Norm leaped off the couch. "DO IT. DO IT. DO IT."

"Sometime in May?"

"Perfect. Splurch.com is moving to San Jose on May 1st.. You can stay here and ride to work with me until you find your own places."

"Do you really think you can get us jobs at splurch.com?"

"I guarantee it."

March 3, 2000

Tech Startups Dangling Huge Pay Packages

CHAOS

Friday * March 10, 2000
7:41 PM

我不在家食晚饭了,嫲嫲.

"I won't be home for dinner, Grandma."

可以食饭了,我和爷爷正等着食饭.

"It's all ready. Your grandfather and I are sitting here waiting."

Milena 准备在星期日离开,我们正帮她准备一切.

"Milena is leaving Sunday and we're still trying to get her ready."

你又再次同那猫太人食饭.

"You're having dinner with that Jewish man again."

我不同 phil steinberg 食饭,那还工作.

"I am not having dinner with Phil Steinberg. I am working."

你的爷爷不喜欢他.

"Your grandfather doesn't like him."

他是白人又是猫太人,这就是他不喜欢他的原因.

"He's a white and he's Jewish. That's why he doesn't like him."

你爷爷想眼你谈下.

"Your grandfather wants to speak to you."

我没有时间.

"I don't have time."

phil 不是个好人.

"Phil is not a good man."

splurch.com

你已经同我讲过了，爷爷.

"You've already told me that, Grandpa."

我再这同你讲.

"I am telling you again."

多谢

"Thank you."

I shouldn't have introduced Phil to my grandparents Holly thought as she put down the receiver.

"There is something wrong with this computer," Milena shouted from her desk on the other side of the loft. "I am leaving to sell splurch.com to the world in thirty-six hours and my computer is broken. Damn. Damn. Damn."

Holly crossed the loft to Milena's desk. "What's wrong?"

"It won't print out. I've tried everything."

"Holly's third law of computers states that all computers will work perfectly until you absolutely can't afford for them to fail."

Unfortunately, Holly's attempt at humor didn't make a dent in Milena's anger. "I need to print out. Now!"

Holly ran through her list of ways to get the words off the monitor and onto the page. Nothing worked.

"Let's get Sal up here," said Milena.

"Excellent idea," said Holly as she ran to the back of the loft and started singing, "Sal...ohhhh Sal...we need you."

Sal yelled back. "I am in the middle of an upload. I'll be there in five minutes."

"Have Norm do it," shouted Milena, "we need you now."

"Norm left for the day," said Holly.

Milena shouted, "Of course Norm left for the day. Does Norm have any stake in the success of a splurch.com IPO? I guess not."

Sal finally came bounding up the circular stairs. "How can I help?"

162

"The printer won't print," said Milena.

"Is it turned on?" asked Sal.

Everyone laughed until they looked at the printer. The green light on the bottom wasn't lit.

Milena grabbed her face in frustration. "Oh MY God. I am an idiot. I unplugged the printer a couple hours ago. I needed to charge my palm pilot and there wasn't an outlet under my desk not being used."

"Happens to all of us," said Sal as he switched on the printer and started back down the stairs.

"Wait," Milena said as she pulled a bottle of wine from under the desk. "Please share a drink with me in retribution for my insanity."

"Sure. It's Friday night and I am on my bike."

Milena pretended to hide the bottle. "We can't have you getting run over by any more busses."

Sal grabbed the bottle, took a swig, and handed it back to Milena. "Hmmmmm."

Holly grabbed the bottle from Milena and also took a swig "Double hmmmmm."

"Aren't you guys worried about germs?" Milena asked.

"We're all in the splurch.com family," said Holly.

"That's right," said Milena as she grabbed the bottle and took a swig. "We should get back to work, but how about another wine summit here in the loft in ninety minutes?"

"That's 9:30," said Holly.

"Great," said Sal.

At 9:30 - on the nose...the three splurchers returned to share the bottle again.

"What are you and Tom doing on the splurch.com Road Show, anyway?" asked Sal.

"Scheduling as many presentations as we can," said Milena.

163

splurch.com

"Why?"

"To convince a bunch of obsessive compulsive twenty-eight year old Ivy League MBAs who are managing more money than God that if they skip the splurch.com IPO their career is over and they'll be lucky to get counter positions at McDonalds."

"What cities are you going to?" asked Sal.

"We just printed out a list," said Holly. "It has all the cities Tom and Milena are traveling to and interesting tidbits on everybody they are meeting - including their favorite color."

"They all like only one color," laughed Milena, "GREEN."

After the wine summit, Sal walked Holly to her bus stop, and they talked about the current status of her billionaire boyfriend.

"He is going too fast for me," laughed Holly.

"Sometimes that's what it takes," muttered Sal mostly to himself.

The bus arrived. Holly got on and he looked out the window as it accelerated. Sal was racing beside the bus. Such a great guy, Holly thought, as she watched Sal pedaled furiously, and then stop, smile, and wave good-bye.

Why wasn't she going out with Sal?

Wonder what her conservative Chinese grandfather would think about a boyfriend from El Salvador?

March 11, 2000

Information Gathered by Web Sites Threatens Personal Privacy

ROAD SHOW

Sunday * March 12, 2000
7:33 AM

CLICK

Milena: This is Milena Peterson, the Chief Executive Officer of
splurch.com. and this is an audio diary of the splurch.com Road Show.
I am sitting at Gate B23 of the San Francisco International Airport.
We've been informed that our flight to New York is going to be
departing three hours later than scheduled. Let's ask Tom Samoley -
our acting Chief Financial Officer - what he thinks of the delay.

Tom: It sucks.

Milena: That's right it sucks and now Tom and I are going to breakfast
at one of the many over-priced restaurants here at SFO. More later.

CLICK

Milena: We are on the plane and winging our way to the financial
capital of the world - the one - the only - New York City. Below us
the snow capped peaks of the Rocky Mountains glisten in the afternoon
sun. We might be flying over Aspen right now. Hello skiers! Tom
Samoley is sitting next to me and is about to call our investment banker,
Joshua Brady, to cancel the late dinner we had scheduled at Tom's
favorite New York restaurant because our stupid plane delay means
we'll get in too late. Let's ask Tom what he thinks.

Tom: It sucks.

Milena: That's right it sucks. More as it happens.

CLICK

Milena: I am now in room 614 at the Regis Hotel in New York City. It's
one o'clock in the morning. It's only ten in San Francisco so that's
probably why I can't sleep. I am prepared for tomorrow's 8 AM presentation at the Prudential Building. I am not nervous. There will be

165

splurch.com

250 hot shot MBA Investment Bankers watching my twenty minute PowerPoint presentation and then asking me God knows what kind of questions. I am not nervous. This is probably the most important day of my life but I am not nervous. Tom and I are meeting in the lobby at 7:30 for a final talk through. I am not nervous. I am not nervous. I am not nervous.

CLICK

Milena: It's three in the morning. Five hours until our first presentation. I can't sleep. Thank God for twenty-four hour room service. Silverware and gorgeous china. Why does the most important presentation have to be on the morning of the first day? Why don't they do it like Broadway shows - perform in the boondocks and ramp up to the Big Apple. Inquiring minds want to know.

CLICK

Milena: It's four a.m. I am sitting at my window watching the rain fall on the city that never sleeps. Beautiful.

CLICK

Milena: We are in the limo on the way to our first presentation. Our driver is Sunil Bathiot. Súnil is from Pakistan. Sunil would you like to say hello to our audio audience?

Sunil: Hello audio audience.

Tom Samoley is sitting next to me. Tom, do you feel confident about our presentation this morning?

Tom: We are going to kick ASSSSS.

CLICK

Milena: The show went great. They loved us. We answered every question. How does the acting Chief Financial Officer think it went?

Tom: We kicked ASSSSSSS.

Milena: We are on our way to our second presentation.

Tom (off mike): We'll have the book done by the end of the week.

Milena: What will splurch.com close at on opening day?

Tom: Over a hundred a share.

Milena: You heard it here first. More as it happens.

CLICK

Milena: Three shows done and miles to go before we sleep. We should probably not count the last presentation. The connection from the lap top to the projector didn't work. So it was only talk and hand outs. I think they hated us and the entire splurch.com concept. There will be no splurch.com stock purchased by these fellows.

Tom (off mike): Those bastards will be begging to get back in the night of the IPO.

CLICK

Milena: Sorry I have not updated you audio diary. This is now day three of the splurch.com Road Show. We are in the limo on our way to our fifteenth presentation. I think it's going well. Any opinion Tom?

Tom: No.

CLICK

Milena: We are now on the plane to London. I have been trying to get some sleep but we've hit turbulence for the last two hours. We get in at six and our first London show will be at nine. That would be four New York time. How will I be able to talk?

CLICK

Milena: London went okay. We could have done better. We have done 37 presentations. We are on our way to Paris. I am a zombie. All I want to do is sleep.

CLICK

Milena: Paris went well. We should make a French version of the splurch.com site. Flying back to the States now. First stop Chicago.

CLICK

Milena: Day seventeen. This is harder than I thought. I really need to sleep.

CAT'S AWAY

⊞

Friday * March 17, 2000
4:33 PM

An orange Nerf ball bounced off Norm's head.

"What the hell is going on?" he shouted.

"Engineering versus sales," Sal yelled from his cubicle three holes down. "We're in trouble. Sales has secured the high ground."

Norm stood up and turned towards the Executive Loft. A pink balloon filled with liquid came flying at him.

Blam!

Direct hit.

"Fuck, Fuck, Fuck," Norm shouted as green liquid dripped down his face and onto his Dancing Pineapple shirt. "This is my brand new Hawaiian shirt. What was in that balloon?"

Holly sprang from behind a filing cabinet and launched two more liquid grenades down towards Norm. "Gatorade!"

"This is a workplace," Norm shouted. He ducked under the folding table on the far side of his cubicle as Gatorade balloons exploded on the floor where he had been standing. "This is totally childish behavior."

"This is war," yelled Sal as he arrived in Norm's cubicle carrying two Super Soakers. "A war that engineering is going to win."

"We have work to do."

"Plenty of time to work," said Sal solemnly. "But if we don't retaliate now we'll never be able to co-exist with sales."

"Somebody could get fired for this," said Norm.

"Who's going to tell?" asked Sal. "Tom and Milena are gallivanting

168

around the world pitching splurch.com and ten minutes ago the last responsible authority figure walked out the front door."

"I'm a responsible authority figure."

"Norm. You're an engineer. You're not a responsible authority figure."

"I am fifty-one years old."

"So?"

Norm took the squirt gun that Sal was handing him. "You're right. Let's get 'em"

The battle raged. Norm and Sal tried to take the loft by charging up the red metal circular stairs but were driven back by Holly and her sales cohorts. When the loft team ran out of water balloons, they started throwing stacks of recycled paper down on their attackers. Sal finally gained the loft and chased Holly down the stairs blasting her with his over sized water gun. As they reached the bottom of the stairs, Holly tripped over Norm's foot and crashed into the Foosball table.

"MY GOD," said Sal throwing down his water gun and tearing down the circular stairs. "Are you okay Holly?"

"I was trying to get out of her way," said Norm as Sal raced past him and knelt beside the unmoving twenty two year old.

Holly opened her eyes and spit a stream of water into Sal's face. "SUCKER."

Sal grabbed Holly and dragged her kicking and screaming toward the splurch.com kitchen. He held her head under the cold water faucet and turned it to full.

"PEACE," sputtered Holly. "THE SPLURCH.COM WAR IS OVER."

Sal immediately turned the water off and offered to shake Holly's hand. The entire office cheered as she ignored the hand and gave Sal a full body hug instead.

"Clean up time," said Holly as she surveyed the devastation around her.

"What about the Foosball table," Sal said holding up a bent Foosball bar missing two of it's wooden warriors.

"Let's buy a new table right now," said Norm. "We can take my car."

splurch.com

As Sal and Holly piled into his front seat of Norm's Mazda and asked, "Where to?"

"Toys 'R Us," said Holly.

"More upscale than that," said Norm. "Let's do this right."

"GO NORM," screamed Holly.

"There's an FAO Schwartz on Stockton right next to Union Square," said Sal.

"Let's go," said Norm.

At FAO Schwartz, the trio purchased a gum ball machine and a top-of-the line Foosball table.

At the check out Holly asked, "How are we paying for this?"

"Pick a card...any card," Norm joked as he pulled four credit cards from his wallet.

"You sure you want to pay for all of it?" asked Sal.

"What's money when you're having so much fun?" asked Norm as he handed his gold Master Card to the check out lady. "I won't have to pay the credit card bill until next month and by then I'll get Milena to reimburse me."

As Norm signed the charge slip, he knew he would never ask Milena for the money. Too much trouble explaining the whys and wherefores. I can afford to do things like this now, he thought. With splurch.com going public I can afford to do a lot of things I couldn't afford before.

DINNER IN DALLAS

$

Monday * March 20, 1999
7:34 PM

"Now THIS is a drink," sighed Gus Jorman as the waitress placed the sixteen ounces of bourbon in front of him. "Honey, you're makin' this cowpoke a happy man."

"You aren't going to drink all that," said Tom Samoley.

"Yes I am," said Gus as he reached over, took Tom's wine glass off the table, and put it on the floor. "And Tom is going to have one too."

"I can't drink that much bourbon."

"Darlin', my partner here wants a Big Burb."

The perky twenty-one year old with the cascading blonde hair and frilly cowgirl vest winked at the silver haired man in the cowboy hat and headed back towards the bar. "Another BB on it's way."

"I can't drink that much bourbon," repeated Tom.

"Yes you can."

"No. I can't."

Gus put his index finger to his lips. "Shhhhhhhh."

Tom silently watched the big breasted cowgirl placed the glass of bourbon in front of him.

"Now let's review our situation here," said Gus. "On April 3rd you are going to be offering splurch.com stock to the public. For the offering to be successful, investment types like myself have to be willing to buy a lot of the stock when it goes on sale. When you leave Dallas tomorrow morning, you'd like to be able to write down in that little book of yours that my associates and I have agreed to buy a whole pile of splurch.com stock for ten dollars a share."

171

splurch.com

"Eleven."

"Ten-fifty."

"Deal," said Tom as he took a sip of bourbon.

"Now, if I was to agree to something nice like that, I would want to be absolutely sure that I have invested in the right company."

"Splurch.com is a great investment because..."

"YEAH YEAH YEAH," Gus cut him off. "You and your spunky CEO already explained all that good investment malarkey to me and my partners...ahhh...what's her name?"

"Milena Peterson.

"Milena's show was very impressive. Pretty slides and the most outrageous income projections I've ever seen."

"Most outrageous income projections you've ever seen?"

"Since that fellow tried to get us to invest in his CD ROM business a few years back."

Tom laughed and took another sip of his Big Burb.

"For the rest of the night, I don't want to hear any of your dot com web internet computer bullshit. What I want, is for you to look me in the eye and say I am not going to lose money on this investment."

"Splurch.com is going to fly. It's got everything. It's got..."

"That's good," said Gus. "But I don't want to hear it now. I want to hear it after you finish your drink. A Big Bourbon works like a truth serum. Kind of like a Q thing in a James Bond movie."

"Q thing?"

"The guy who made all those gadgets for 007."

"Oh yeah," said Tom taking another small sip of his drink. "You know I have to fly to Chicago tomorrow morning at eight o'clock. I have nine presentations in the next three days. I can't drink this much Bourbon."

"Your father ever tell ya how he got me to invest in his video biz?"

"No."

"Twenty years ago, he was sitting right there in the seat that you are sitting in now."

"In this bar?"

"It was the night we invented the Big Burb. Drink up son."

Tom took a long swallow and decided not to fight it. There was only a week left of splurch.com .shows and maybe he could afford to let his hair down for one night.

"While you're drinking up, could you please explain to me why both our towns have such lousy basketball teams," said a smiling Gus.

"The Mavericks aren't as bad as the Warriors."

"The Clippers beat us by thirty points last week."

"That hurts."

"I think it might have to do with Don Nelson. Some kind of bad voodoo."

"You could be right."

An hour later, Gus and Tom were debating whether Joe Montana was actually throwing the ball out of the end zone on *The Catch,* and two hours later they were reciting historic Bill Murray lines to each other and ordering a third round of Big Burbs instead of dinner.

Tom never got around to looking Gus in the eye and telling him that he wouldn't lose money if he invested in splurch.com.

GOLDEN GATE BRIDGE

Friday * March 24, 2000
6:06 PM

"We're walking all the way across the bridge?"

"And back," laughed Holly as she leaped off the last step of the 29 Sunset bus and headed towards the stone wall overlooking Fort Point and San Francisco Bay.

Sal climbed off the bus and stood beside Holly absorbing the post card views in every direction.

"Thank you Sal for doing this with me," Holly said. "I've wanted to hike across the Golden Gate Bridge for such a long time."

"No problem."

"Perfect timing. Clear weather and a setting sun."

"Known as Magic Hour in the world of film."

"You learn that helping on the splurch.com commercial?"

"That, and many other things, including what a CFU is."

"What's a CFU?"

"A CFU means Camera Fuck Up. It's when the camera goes out of focus or doesn't do exactly what the director wants. It's different from a SFU which means Sound Fuck Up, or an AFU which means Actor Fuck Up. The first ten takes that Don Johnson did were AFU's."

"Why did he screw up so much? He's a pro."

"He was having fun, screwing around, and giving the director fits."

"And making Tom Samoley crazy."

"Probably the main reason."

"Seen the commercial yet?"

"I taped Dawson's Creek and when I got home last night I checked the tape and there it was."

"Any good?"

"Interesting," said Sal as they headed to the bridge. "You want to come by my place after our hike and see it for yourself?"

"Sounds like a plan Stan."

"Great."

"Click. Wrrrrr." Holly began walking backwards and moving her head in slow circles. "Click. Wrrrr. Click Wrrrr."

"What are you doing?"

"Taking mental pictures."

"There's a store back in the parking lot. I'll go buy one of those instant cameras," said Sal.

"Don't do that," said Holly grabbing Sal's arm and turning him towards her. "This is much better. Click. Wrrrrr." Holly was now looking directly into his eyes. "Click. Wrrrrr. I'll never lose these pictures."

A half hour later, Sal and Holly reached the far side of the bridge and flopped down the large stone benches on the overlook. They lay on their backs and watched the blazing red clouds race across the sky.

"Click. Wrrrrr."

"Good pictures?" asked Sal.

"The best. Click. Wrrrrr."

Sal looked at the clouds and thought about how much he liked Holly. She was smart, fun, and beautiful. She was everything he could ever want in a woman. But they were just friends. He guessed that was okay. Better to be friends than nothing. Right. Right Sal? He was too damn shy. No. He was too damn chicken to tell her how much he liked her.

"What's the latest with Phil?" he finally blurted out.

"Complicated. Click. Wrrrrr."

"I hear he named his boat the Holly Dream."

"Correct."

"He still wants to marry you?"

"Correct."

"Are you going to marry him?"

"Not tonight. Click. Wrrrrr."

Sal squeezed his eyes tight and her words screamed in his head - NOT TONIGHT. What the hell did that mean?

When Sal opened his eyes, Holly had left the bench and was talking to a couple standing at the wall watching a container ship slide under the Golden Gate Bridge. They were telling her about their farm back in Audubon, Iowa and ended up offering Holly and Sal a ride back across the bridge in their rental car.

"Shall we take a raincheck on our return hike?" Holly asked Sal.

"It will be pitch black by the time we got back across anyway."

In the car, Holly told the Iowans about splurch.com and asked them to join her and Sal for a drink at the Wishing Well in the Inner Sunset. Everyone bought a round, and then Holly suggested they head to Sal's apartment to check out the splurch.com television commercial.

"Messy, messy, messy," chanted Sal as they climbed the stairs to his apartment.

"Don't care. Don't care. Don't care," Holly and her Midwestern pals responded.

"I have a six pack in the fridge."

"Yeah," everyone cheered.

They all drank a beer and then watched the commercial. When the commercial ended, nobody said anything. Sal rewound the tape and they watched it again.

"It's different," said the Iowa man finally.

"I sure like Don Johnson," said the Iowa woman. "He's great in Nash Bridges."

"I like Cheech better," said Holly.

After a twenty minute discussion on television stars, the Iowa couple left.

Holly and Sal had another beer and smoked some pot that Sal had been saving.

Then they kissed.

Then they kissed again.

March 27 2000

Former GM Exec
Leads Web Venture

SILICON SILENCE

Monday * March 27, 2000
7:03 AM

Holly sat in a blue plastic chair and watched the man she'd been chatting with - a great looking guy with a razor cut and perpetual smile - open the door to release the parade of exhausted humans into the terminal.

Milena and Tom were the third and fourth people to stumble through the door. Immediate escape from the airplane squeeze box had to be one of the most important first class perks, thought Holly.

"Thank God," Milena said as soon as she saw Holly, "a friendly face."

"Is the limo waiting?" barked Tom.

"At the curb," Holly said as they walked briskly towards baggage.

"Why did we schedule a show in Sydney," mumbled Tom. "That was stupid. Who cares about Australian investors."

"I thought it went well," said Milena.

"If our final California shows don't wow 'em we're in big trouble."

"Don't worry. You'll wow 'em," chirped Holly. "Tom and Milena are two wowing kind of people."

Tom gave her "that" look and Holly decided she'd better not make any more cute comments.

No one talked in the limo. Holly glanced into the rear view mirror as the two exhausted executives slumped on opposite sides of the seat. Milena had on more make-up than usual but looked ten years older. Tom grimaced as nightmare visions tripped on the inside of his clenched eye lids.

The Palo Alto presentation was scheduled for 8:00, but didn't start

178

until 8:20 because the guy that usually lowered the auditorium screen didn't show up for work. Milena's PowerPoint presentation went flawlessly and most of the question and answers were about how splurch.com was going to be "first mover" in the "space" they "occupied." Who cares, thought Holly. Splurch.com is either going to attract people, clients, and advertising or it won't - these bullshit investors were making it way too complicated.

"So what did you think of our little splurch.com show?" Milena asked as the limo raced to their next stop.

"Splurch.com is a winner. I want to invest right now."

Milena laughed. Tom didn't.

The San Mateo show was scheduled at noon, but the limo didn't pull into the massive parking lot until 11:55. Milena and Tom raced out of the car and started the show at 12:07. Milena stumbled in her presentation, the PowerPoint crashed, and all the question were about patent infringement. Tom tried to explain that the rights weren't a problem, but Holly could tell by the tone of the questions that nobody in the room was convinced.

"Do you want to be a CEO like Milena when you grow up?" Tom asked Holly as they drove to the next show.

"I'm never going to grow up," said Holly.

"Don't tell anybody what you heard today," said Tom firmly.

"Why?" Holly laughed.

Tom didn't say anything. He just gave her "that" look again.

Milena asked Tom a question about the patent. Tom patted Milena's head and told her not to worry. Holly bit her lip and didn't say anything. She hated the head patting thing and Tom did it all the time. What was the deal - did he think women were dogs?

The San Francisco auditorium was packed, but, ten minutes into the presentation, Staner Lipton appeared and everyone stopped paying attention to Milena. Tom invited Staner to the stage and, for the rest of the meeting, Staner answered questions about the future of technology and what Bill Gates was really like. Tom and Staner went to dine at Vertigo and Holly and Milena headed back to the limo.

Milena explained the importance of the quiet period for the IPO and Holly said she would surround herself with a wall of silicon silence until April 3rd. Milena pulled out the back seat bar and made them both drinks. She took off her pumps, leaned her head on the back of the seat, and said, "so what do you think?"

"About what?"

"About anything."

"I think Tom Samoley is a patronizing asshole."

"That's for sure."

"I think you're working way too hard."

"That's for sure."

"Riding in a limo with a little television and free drinks is total fun."

"I've ridden in so many limos that the thrill is totally gone."

"I think that's too bad."

"I think you're right."

IPO

Monday * April 3, 2000
6:47 AM

SPRC @ $10.25 (Opening Bell)

Milena stared at the screen. Splurch.com was finally being offered to the world. As the price for the rest of the one thousand eight hundred and seventy NASDAQ companies crawled across the bottom of her screen, Milena heaved a sigh of relief. She had done it. Splurch.com was going public.

SUNM (Sun Microsystems) appeared at 26.50. That means, an investor who wanted to buy stock this morning could buy one hundred shares of Scott McNealy's dream for about the same price he could buy two hundred shares of Milena Peterson's dream.

Time to call Mom.

SPRC @ $13.10 (Twenty Minutes After Opening Bell)

"Up another ten cents," Milena said into the phone.

"Wonderful dear," said Justine Peterson in her overly relaxed telephone style.

"I just made five thousand dollars in twenty minutes."

"Oh my."

"And I didn't have to do anything. Just sit here and drink coffee."

"You put in an awful lot of time and energy getting splurch.com to this point."

"Every waking minute of the last eighteen months."

"And you'll be putting in more time in the future."

"Every waking minute for the rest of my life," laughed Milena.

181

"It's not easy money."

"Yeah, but it sure feels easy now."

"Does this mean you'll not have time to come and visit your dear old mother in Florida?"

"I promise I'll get there sometime in the next couple months. I think there's a software convention in Orlando around March 1st."

"You owe me," said Justine. "Not coming for Christmas was not good for your mom's status in her West Palm hide-away. None of my pals believe that this fabulous daughter of mine - the one that I have been bragging about for the last year - the one that is taking over Silicon Valley - actually exists."

"I'll come."

"Promise."

"Yes."

"Cross your heart and hope to die?"

"Yes."

"Are you doing it?"

"Doing what?"

"Crossing your heart?"

"I am crossing my heart, but I am not hoping to die."

"Have you talked to your father yet?"

"You're my first call."

"When you talk to my ex-husband, could you please say hello from me?"

"A friendly hello or an angry hello?"

"A neutral hello."

"Will do."

SPRC @ 18.10 (One Hour After Opening Bell)

"Hey Dad."

"It's going up."

"You've been watching it?"

"Since the opening."

"My Dad cares."

"Yes, your Dad cares. I set up my NBCi home page so that the splurch.com stock price comes on automatically right next to the weather."

"Great."

"And I am going to sit here all day and watch it go up."

"No golf today?"

"I can miss one day of golf for this."

"Tomorrow you could take your palm pilot to the links and watch the splurch.com stock go up between holes."

"No. I want to have something to look forward to after the game - especially if I lose."

"Not likely."

"I am getting old. Not as many yards on my drives."

"If splurch.com gets past fifty will you change your mind about dot com investments."

"Nope. I'm staying with WalMart and General Electric."

"Do you have those stocks on your home page?"

"Don't need to. They don't change much."

"That's good?"

"Yes. That's good."

"How can you say that when I'm making so much money today?"

"It's just on paper. You haven't made any real money yet."

"How about one hundred and eighty days from now, when I cash in a small portion of my wealth and buy you a new set of golf clubs. Will you then admit the new economy has some reality to it?"

"Throw in dinner and it's a deal."

"Deal," laughed Milena and then quietly said, "give Mom a call."

"I called her last month."

"Call her again."

"Your will is my command."

SPRC @ $ 47.50 (Three Hours After Opening Bell)

When Milena walked into the splurch.com office, everyone was gathered around computer screens watching the splurch.com price skyrocket.

"Explain this right now," said Holly as she came running down the circular staircase. "How rich am I?"

"How many options do you have?"

"Five hundred."

"What's your option price?"

"Ten dollars."

"What is the splurch.com price now?"

"Just hit SIXTY," yelled Sal from a group huddled around the receptionist's computer.

Another cheer echoed through the office as Milena put her arm around Holly. "You made twenty-five thousand dollars today."

Holly gasped and started a splurch.com cheer.

"Give me an S."

The entire office roared, "S."

POT OF GOLD

Monday * April 3, 2000
7:22 PM

As soon as the phone picked up Norm screamed, "Did you see where splurch.com closed today?"

"Seventy-five."

"Correct o' brother of mine. So guess how much I made in one day."

"Ten million dollars."

"Correct."

There was a pause. "I was joking," Chris finally said.

"I'm not," said Norm.

"You made ten million dollars today?"

"Your brother is now a multi-millionaire."

Chris whistled and then asked, "are you passing some of that cash on to your siblings?"

"Better than that. I talked to Milena and got you and Sarah both jobs. When you get here - you're hired."

"We'll give notice tomorrow."

"Ha Ha."

"I am not joking. We've wasted too much time in the land of cold and limited opportunities. I am calling Sarah as soon as we hang up."

Norm sighed. "That would be great."

Norm said goodbye and switched on his computer. As it booted up, he thought about how great it was going to be to work in the same company with his brother and sister. Thank God for the new economy. Thank God for splurch.com. Was there any difference between the Gold Rush in '49 and the Dot Com Rush in '99? Yep. There was more gold in the web biz than anyone could pull out of the ground in a million years.

For the next hour, Norm enjoyed his new prosperity. He bought over sixty-five thousand dollars in computer parts and electronic toys on-line. Before the IPO, adding that much to his credit card balance would have been a major trauma. Today, it was such a small part of his total worth it hardly seemed significant. He wasn't being extravagant. He had been researching the purchases for months. He did indulge himself a little. For every purchase, no matter what kind of outrageous charge the retailer happened to be charging, Norm hit the immediate delivery option.

Norm ordered dinner from La Foret. The duck, the salmon, and the Kobi steak. Hmmmmmm hmmmm good. The restaurant, which didn't normally deliver, told him they would arrange to have the food delivered by taxi when Norm said they could add a hundred and fifty dollar tip to the credit card charge.

Norm called Sal. After one ring, Sal picked up. "Fun Central."

"Is that you Sal?"

"The one and only. This sounds like my computer compatriot, Norman Dotoshay. To what do I owe the pleasure of this analog connection?"

"Could you cover for me for the first couple hours tomorrow morning?"

"I cover for you every minute of every day at the splurch.com factory," laughed Sal. "Why would tomorrow morning be any different?"

"If Milena comes hunting for me, cut her off at the pass, okay?"

"Don't worry. Tomorrow morning, Milena will still be in euphoria land from the splurch.com price explosion - especially if the stock continues to keep climbing. A few hours of No Norm isn't going to bother her."

"Spend any of your money yet?"

"What money?"

"From your splurch.com options?"

"It's not real yet."

"It will be."

"My money won't be real in a hundred and eighty days like yours."

"How long do you have to wait?"

"A year."

"No problem. A year from now the splurch.com price will double."

"Or drop below fifty."

"Don't say such things. You'll screw the pooch."

"Screw the pooch - what the hell does that mean?"

"Old time astronaut talk."

"So what is my engineering buddy doing tomorrow morning that is so important he can't show up for work at the most highly valued dot com in the universe?"

"When I get there, you'll know."

Norm clicked off and decided it was time to make his big on-line purchase. Having lots of money was only fun if it brought you total joy. What good was a long list of numbers in a bank account? The pleasure was buying something you really wanted. Norm could now afford to make his dreams come true. He went to the web site and started the process of buying his dream. He filled out the financial forms, checked the color he wanted, and listed every option on his new Beemer. He hit send and within ten minutes was informed that he could pick up the exact car he wanted at a BMW dealership in Los Gatos the next day.

This truly was an age when dreams come true.

LOAN

$

Thursday * April 6, 2000
4:48 PM

Tom looked at the document and smiled. He wanted to extend this moment as long as possible. "I guess we have an agreement," he finally said.

"If you sign," said the banker with the Italian accent and the shiny Gucci suit that was holding a Waterman pen towards him.

"Let me think," said Tom scratching his head. "Why didn't you people want to loan me this money last week?"

"We would have loaned this money to you last week."

"You were saying yes but your terms were saying - no way - get out of here - take a hike bozo."

The banker frowned and then smiled, "You are making joke."

"Does splurch.com's successful public offering have anything to do with the wonderful terms you are now offering me?"

"I am not sure what you are asking."

"You don't have to tell me because I know the answer. The current pile of splurch.com money doesn't have anything to do with the terms you are now offering. It has everything to do with it." Tom came around the desk and pulled up a chair next to the startled banker. "Let's see where old splurch.com is now. Can you get stock prices on this computer?"

"Of course."

"Pull up SPRC."

The banker hit some keys and the splurch.com price appeared.

"Look at that," exclaimed Tom, "It's at $85 a share. Is that why you're now willing to loan me the money I need for half the rate you were trying to screw me with last week?"

Tom grabbed the pen and started signing the documents. "This money will be available as soon as I walk out the door?"

"I am afraid that's impossible."

Tom stopped in mid-signature and looked at the banker. "When will it be available?"

"Would tomorrow morning when the bank opens be suitable?"

"Not suitable - but I'll live with it."

When Tom got into his Ferrari, he called the splurch.com media buyer and doubled the television buy. The commercial was just too good to not be seen by the entire world. The buyer said that the networks were now demanding cash up front for those kind of change orders. He told her it was not a problem. The iron was hot - it was time to strike.

Tom called the splurch.com Board members and left messages playfully reminding all of them of the Board meeting coming up, and adding a personal touch to each.

Horace Krennan: "All systems go. Splurch.com is set to soar."

Jerry Tenther: "Remember Apple in '86? Splurch.com is going to be bigger than that. No kidding."

Clary Wathers III: "We are now winning bigtime. I guess if you roll the dice enough times you eventually come up with a winner like splurch.com."

Hernando Formento: "Hope you have some dancing girls standing by."

Staner Lipton: "I have a way for you to make up for your accountant screwing up our Aspen deal. You star in the next splurch.com television commercial. What do you think?"

When Tom walked into splurch.com, the former auto parts warehouse filled with cheers. He ran up the circular stairs yelling, "Milena, it's celebration dinner time."

splurch.com

Milena didn't look up from her computer as Tom reached the loft. "Sounds great. We'll go as soon as I finish this report."

"Going now," said Tom as he lifted Milena's hands off her keyboard. He pulled out his cell phone and dramatically turned it off, "No cell phones tonight either. We're doing this dinner right.

Tom and Milena had a great dinner. The tension was over. The splurch.com Road Show had worked. They were now a team to be reckoned with all across dot com land. Splurch.com was a success and their Silicon Valley futures were secure.

After dinner, Tom dropped Milena at her car and bellowed out Temptations hits for the entire drive back the to Woodside. The sky was clear. The moon was full.

When he walked into his home office the answering machine was flashing.

"This is Biz Dufkin from the San Jose Mercury News. I just wanted to let you know that we're running a story about patent infringement in tomorrow's paper. The charges against splurch.com are pretty serious and I was hoping to get a comment from you or Milena Peterson before we run the story, but I had no luck reaching either of you at your offices or on your cells. If you'd like to talk about it, please give me a call tonight before ten.

Tom looked at his watch. It was 11:19.

CRASH

Thursday * April 13, 2000
7:34 AM

Sal swung into Sally's for his morning coffee and thought about life at splurch.com. Ever since the patent infringement story, things had gotten stranger and stranger. As he locked up his new carbon fibre wheels - his only extravagance against the pile of splurch.com money that everyone assured him would soon be flowing his way - he decided the moon & star alignment must be totally out of wack.

"Is it true?" asked a Sally's regular as Sal walked in. "Did splurch.com steal all its technology?"

"No," said Sal. He stepped to the end of the caffeine line. "It's a just a pile of press bullshit."

The first day everyone at splurch.com had figured the patent infringement story would just fade away, but it had gotten bigger and bigger. Splurch.com was looking more and more like the Darth Vader of the web world. At the company meeting, Milena said the bad press was because the people attacking splurch.com had a better public relations firm. Judging by the inflammatory comments attributed to Tom Samoley every day in the newspaper, Sal figured splurch.com had no public relations people handling spin control.

"So what's going on?" a smiling programmer asked Sal.

"The little guys are trying to get some of the splurch.com bucks. It's the law of the jungle. Lions are always fending off little creatures trying to get a bite of the kill. Microsoft has the same kind of problems."

"What bucks?" asked a pony tailed engineer at the corner table.

"Somebody hasn't been paying attention," said Sal. "Splurch.com went public last week and we raised a boat load of money."

"That boat is sinking fast," said Ponytail as he held up the front page

splurch.com

of the *San Francisco Chronicle*.

STOCK MARKET CRASH
STEEPEST DECLINE IN NASDAQ HISTORY

Splurch.com one of new issues hit hard.

Sal stared at the paper and mumbled to himself, "Oh my God."

When Sal walked into the office, he was greeted with a loud crash. He looked up to see Tom Samoley picking up another phone to toss after the one he had just thrown from the Exectuive Loft. Sal put his bike on his shoulder and tried to quietly sneak towards his cubicle. Milena spotted him. She was gripping the loft railing so tight her fingers were turning white. She whispered softly, "The web site is down again."

Tom threw the second phone to the floor and screamed, "WHY IS THE FUCKING SITE DOWN AGAIN?"

Sal stared at the two insane dot com executives and said quietly, "I don't know."

"Why didn't you return our page?" Milena asked.

"I lost my pager a couple of days ago."

"FIND THE FUCK OUT WHY THE SITE IS DOWN AND GET IT BACK THE FUCK UP," shouted Tom as he picked up a small silver waste basket and threw it to the warehouse floor.

When Sal got to his cubicle, Holly was sitting in his chair sobbing.

"I am sorry Sal," she cried. "I had to go somewhere and hide. Milena called me at 6:30 this morning to tell me the site was down and that the stock price had dropped thirty dollars in twenty minutes. She asked me to come in and I did. But there is nothing I can do. I can't fix the site and sitting there watching the stock drop with those two was too painful."

"When it rains it pours," said Sal as he hung his bike on the wall.

"I tried to call ya," said Holly. "No answer."

"I wish I'd been there." Sal booted up his computer and started trying to figure out why splurch.com wasn't splurching this morning. "I'm doing an hour long bike ride every morning before work to get in shape."

"Maybe I should join you."

"That would be great."

Sal had the site up and running in thirty minutes.

Norm arrived after ten. He had been in a traffic jam and is cell phone battery had died. He had no idea about the splurch.com stock price drop or the broken web site.

The profanity that Tom sprayed at Norm when he walked in the front door was truly breathtaking.

At the end of the day, Milena stopped at Sal's cubicle to apologize for her rude morning behavior. Sal told Milena not to worry and asked what the price drop would actually mean to the future of splurch.com. She said she didn't know. Sal handed her the invoice he had just gotten from the hospital. She glanced at it and said, "this is not something I want to think about right now."

Sal sat in his cubicle holding the bill as Milena left to climb the circular staircase to her Executive Loft.

I guess a hundred and thirty thousand dollars isn't that important when we're talking millions, thought Sal.

April 13, 2000

NASDAQ Bombs

REALITY CHECK

Friday * April 14, 2000
6:18 AM

The laughter of the KFOG morning show filled the bedroom. Milena hit the snooze bar and, again, Dave Morey stopped talking. This time, however, the splurch.com CEO was unable to escape back into her dream world. A world where the price of splurch.com stock was still soaring, the web site was still functioning, and there was no press proclaiming splurch.com the Saddam Hussein of the Bay Area. Consciousness gained the upper hand, and the reality of the dot com hell she was living in slowly permeated her entire being.

What happened?

How could things have changed so much in so short period of time?

What had she done wrong?

Milena decided to stay in bed today. She would just stare out her window at Alcatraz: the abandoned island prison in the middle of San Francisco Bay. Maybe they would turn Alcatraz into a debtor's prison and incarcerate her and all the other dot com executives that had lost their stockholders so much money in the last couple of days. The more she thought about it, the better it sounded. Three squares a day and somebody else to figure out how to drag the stock out of the gutter.

The phone rang. Milena tried to force herself back to sleep. The machine would get it.

The ringing continued. Damn. She must have forgotten to turn the answering machine on after listening to all those horrible messages last night. She got out of bed and checked the caller ID.

Justine Peterson.

She picked up. Maybe her Mom still loved her.

"Hi Mom."

Words and emotions came pouring across the phone line. "I am so glad you picked up Milena. I've been worried sick about you. Your Dad called and told me things weren't going well for splurch.com. Are you alright?"

"I am still walking and talking."

"What happened?"

"I wish I knew," sighed Milena. "Before I start my tale of woe, why don't you tell me what you've been up to."

"Pretty much the same. Playing golf and swimming every day. The latest crisis is my friend Caroline. Do you remember her? You met her the last time you were here."

"Doesn't ring a bell."

"She was drinking out of the Snoopy glass and telling you knock knock jokes at the pool party."

"Oh yeah. I remember her."

"Her husband died six months ago, and she hasn't been the same since. She forgets things. She's scared of being alone at night. We've all been trying to help her but yesterday, her son said he was putting her in a nursing home."

"Oh my," said Milena. Her splurch.com troubles quickly shifted into perspective. Thank you Mom.

"Your turn," Justine said. "Do you still have enough money to buy groceries?"

"Money isn't the problem," laughed Milena. "We have over a hundred million dollars in the bank."

"That will buy a lot of groceries," said Justine. "Why did your Dad tell me you were having such a hard time?"

"Our stock went south and all the stockholders are blaming me."

"What happened?"

"Last week, some financial gurus started whispering that technology stocks might not be such a good idea. People started selling and the companies listed in the NASDAQ - the main place you go to buy and sell technical stock - started losing value. More investors panicked and sold their stock - more panic, more selling, more panic, and...CRASH!"

"Oh my."

"The same day NASDAQ crashed, the splurch.com site crashed. Both have been crashing every day since."

"Has your stock gone down a lot?"

"At one point, splurch.com sold for ninety-three dollars a share. It's now selling for three."

"What happened to the original investors?"

"Most of those rats abandoned SS splurch as soon as we started leaking."

"What do you mean?"

"They all sold their stock as soon as the price started south."

"Did you sell your shares."

"I can't. I'm in lock up. I have to wait six months after the IPO to sell any of it."

"Sounds complicated."

"We're also having a public relations nightmare. Some goofball is claiming he invented the stuff that makes our site go. The press is supporting his small guy claim against us."

"You do own it, right?"

"I thought so. But now I am not so sure."

"I think a hundred million dollars could solve your problems.

"That's what Tom Samoley thinks. He's outlining a new action plan at lunch."

"Good luck. I'll keep my fingers crossed for splurch.com."

"Better keep your toes crossed too."

THROWING MONEY

Friday * April 14, 2000
11:39 AM

"What do you think, Holly?"

Holly stared at Tom on the other side of the elegant table at the XYZ Bistro and gulped. What could she possibly say about the plan for splurch.com that Tom had just described. Holly turned to Milena who was focused on the complex task of extracting white meat from her lobster claw and offered no help.

"It might work," Holly finally said.

"Might work," shouted Tom. "It will work. It'll work like gangbusters. The American public believes what they see on TV and when they see our commercial every time they turn on the idiot box they'll be convinced splurch.com is a brand they can count on. It will be burned into the national consciousness just like McDonald's and Coke."

"Those companies run a variety of different commercials," said Milena. "Not the same spot over and over."

"That's the beauty of my marketing plan," said Tom. "We won't be diluting our message. We'll just keep pounding away with the same thirty second spot. Do you remember the Topol toothpaste commercial?"

Tom looked straight at Holly and she quickly shook her head no. Thank God she had no idea what Topol was and that Tom hadn't directly asked her what she thought of his stupid, incomprehensible splurch.com television commercial.

"Of course not," laughed Tom. "That was long before your time. You were probably still in diapers."

Milena held her napkin in front of her face, blew into it, and then held it to the side and said seriously, "See this ugly yellow stain?"

197

"But LOOK here's Topol!" laughed Tom as he turned to Holly. "See, Milena and I remember every word of that commercial. It's burned in our brains. I just read an article that said, when Topol ran that spot their sales skyrocketed. When they tried a new commercial, sales dropped, so they went back to the original spot and sales took off again."

"They ran the spot on small stations at odd hours," said Milena.

"They didn't have the money to run on network prime time like we do," smiled Tom.

"Is the Board going to agree to this risky expenditure of our entire war chest?" asked Milena.

Tom took a sip of his wine and said, "You and I are going to convince them. It's the fastest way to get the stock price back up to where it should be."

Holly focused on her salmon and tried to figure out why Tom had insisted that she come to this lunch.

"You're probably wondering why I wanted you here," said Tom as he winked at Holly.

Oh no, Holly thought. Are people born with silver spoons in their mouth also born with mind reading capabilities?

"Actually," said Milena, "I was wondering why you wanted Holly here."

"She's going to be our eyes and ears on this campaign," said Tom. "I am going to give her a schedule of when and where the commercial is suppose to run and she's going to watch to make sure that it's on when they say it's on and help us figure out what kind of programs it works best in."

"You want me to watch that commercial every time it's on," said Holly trying to not let her revulsion rise to the surface.

"Right."

"Do I make any extra money for this scouting effort?"

"Five dollars an hour," laughed Tom. "We can afford that, don't you think Milena?"

198

"We can afford almost anything," said Milena. She then whispered under her breath, "at least for awhile."

"Can the official splurch.com commercial eyes and ears ask the acting Chief Financial Officer something?"

"Shoot" said Tom.

"There was another article about splurch.com stealing technology in this morning's paper. My friends are starting to wonder if I work for the forces of evil."

"Problem solved," said Tom. "We're going to give that guy twenty million dollars to go away."

"WHAT!" yelled Milena and started choking on her lobster. "We're right and he's wrong. We could litigate him to death. That's what we agreed to do."

"We're building a brand," Tom said as he reached over and touched Milena's hand. "Image is everything."

"But what happens when our brand runs out of money?"

"Let me worry about that," said Tom patting Milena's hand. "Have you decided when to tell Norm?"

Milena took her hand away. "I don't think it's the right time yet."

"Let's not wait too much longer," said Tom sternly. He suddenly realized that Holly was sitting there and raised his voice sharply. "Not a word about this, Holly."

Holly's insides were churning. Not a word about what?

CHANGES

Tuesday * April 18, 1999
2:19 PM

Milena glanced at the letter and handed it back to Sal.

"I am sorry this has gotten so screwed up," she sighed. "We were in the middle of changing health carriers when you were hit by that bus. Both the new and old insurance companies are claiming that the other company was insuring us at the time of your accident. So both are refusing to pay your hospital and doctor bills."

Sal stared at Milena and then down at the letter informing him that if he didn't make arrangements to pay the one hundred and thirty thousand dollars, the bill would be sent to a collection agency.

"I don't understand," he mumbled, "how could this happen?"

"That's insurance companies for ya. What are you going to do? They rake in as much as they can and then try to pay out as little as humanly possible."

"Am I going to have to pay this bill myself?" Sal asked softly.

"Don't worry." Milena turned towards her computer screen and typed a cryptic reply to an e-mail that had just appeared on her screen. "We'll keep working on your problem 'til it's solved."

"In two weeks they're going to send this bill to a collection agency. If they do that, won't my credit rating be ruined?"

"Sallllll." Milena stopped multi-tasking and focused her executive power gaze directly on him. "Don't worry. You are too valuable an employee for us to muck up. I'll get Holly to yank their chain."

"A hundred and thirty thousand dollars is a lot of money."

"Not as much as you're going to get when you cash in your splurch.com stock options."

200

"I can't do that for a long time, and doesn't the stock have to get back up to a price like it was before?"

"It will. All tech stocks go down and then back up. It's happened so many times before. The NASDAQ falls and then it climbs back up even higher."

"Hope so," Sal said as he headed for the circular stairs.

"Wait. I forgot to thank you for stepping in to solve our daily crash trauma."

"No problem."

"You keep an eye on the site, okay."

"I don't need to. Norm has it under control."

"I don't care. I want you to double check everything. We can't afford to have the site go down for one more minute."

"Okay."

When Sal reached the bottom of the stairs, Holly came racing through the front door with a cardboard box filled with four color splurch.com promotional brochures. Sal playfully blocked Holly's way to the stairs. She got by him with a spin move, but when she reached the first step, he caught her by the belt.

"Mr. Zaldivar. If I don't get this box up to the command center in the next two minutes the entire splurch.com operation will crumble."

Sal released Holly's belt, and she went tearing up the stairs. She stopped halfway and turned back to Sal. "Doing anything tonight?"

"No."

"Want to come over and help me with my splurch.com commercial reporting job."

"Your what?"

"Big new splurch.com TV buy starts tonight."

"What are you talking about?"

"Be at my apartment at 6:45 and I'll explain all."

"Okay."

"Don't be late. The fun starts at seven."

Sal arrived at Holly's apartment at exactly 6:45. She explained the splurch.com commercial assignment Tom had saddled her with, and produced a large bottle of red wine to help dull the pain.

The splurch.com commercial was on twice during the Channel Two Seinfeld re-run. Holly explained that according to Tom's schedule those commercials weren't part of the national buy. They were just part of a local Bay Area buy. It was a good Seinfeld episode. The first Soup Nazi.

When they finished the bottle of wine, Holly produced a joint she had rolled earlier in case they needed more pain dulling medication. They both agreed they needed additional medicine to deal with the splurch.com commercial.

The first national spot ran during the second Dharma and Greg break. Dharma explained to Greg why he had to go to the bakery boycott with her - the screen went dark - and the splurch.com commercial came on. Impressive.

During the next program, the commercial ran in the middle of long group of spots between the last segment of the show and the closing credits. Not as impressive.

Sal suggested they record the next show and check the tape later to see when the commercial ran. Holly immediately agreed.

As Sal was leaving, they hugged and Holly said, "Have you ever thought about us being more than friends?"

Sal gulped. "The thought never crossed my mind."

REUNION

Friday * April 21, 2000
3:22 PM

"I CAN'T BELIEVE IT," Norm shouted for the fourth time in a row. "The Dotoshays all working for the same company. This is too good to be true."

"It's not official yet," said Chris from the shotgun seat of Norm's sleek new BMW.

"They have to offer us jobs first," said Sarah as she leaned in from the back seat and put an arm around both her brothers.

"Get a seatbelt on gal," Norm said as he roared out of the San Francisco Airport and onto 101. "We're going to be doin' some drivin'."

As Norm accelerated north, Chris announced, "Thirty miles per hour over the speed limit is a very expensive ticket."

"You don't know about the new LAW?" laughed Norm.

"Tell us about the new LAW," both siblings said in unison.

"If you're caught speeding, you tell the California State Trooper that you work for a dot com and he's required by..."

"...LAW..." all three Dotoshay's screamed.

"...to let you off with only a warning, IF you offer him enough stock options."

Laughter filled the car as Norm continued to accelerate towards San Francisco.

"How does Mr. Traffic Officer know if your options are worth anything?" asked Sarah as she buckled up.

"I know the answer to that question," volunteered Chris. "All state trooper cars have computers. The officer just goes back to his vehicle

203

and logs onto a web site for some instant analysis. He would check out www.SiliconInvestor.com...or www.thestandard.com...or www.wallstreetjournal.com."

"You have to pay for the journal site," injected Sarah.

"State troopers make good money. They can afford to pay for investment information," Norm said as he raced past the baseball park formerly known as Candlestick.

"Are we going to stop at splurch.com?" asked Chris.

"No way. I keeping you two under wraps. I talked to Milena about the possibility of your coming out, but I am waiting for the perfect opportunity to announce that I actually convinced you to move here and she now has two more totally dependable people she can count on to turn splurch.com into the best dot com in the universe."

"Don't you have to check on how things are going today on the site?" asked Sarah.

"That's why cell phones were invented," said Norm as he pulled out his cell and punched in a number.

"Hey Sal. This is your commander calling," Norm said winking at Chris and Sarah. "Not Tom Samoley. Your tech commander. NORM!"

Norm shook his head in mock frustration and then laughed. "Of course I knew you were kidding." Norm took the Mission Street exit and swooped into San Francisco. "Everything under control at splurch.com. Great. That top secret package I was telling you about arrived safely. I am taking them to dinner and then a show at the Golden Gate Theater. Don't tell anybody."

The Dotoshays dined at Fior D' Italia. Norm ordered so he could demonstrate how well he remembered what they both liked to eat. Of course he mixed up the fish and the shrimp. Chris was the shrimp and Sarah the fish. Dang. When the dishes arrived, they traded dishes and everyone was happy. Norm also insisted on picking up the bill and added a $125 tip to the credit card slip.

"You're not rich yet," warned Sarah.

"Life is short. Better enjoy it while you have the opportunity. Am I right Chris?"

"Sounds like a new LAW."

"Right! From now on, having fun and not worrying about money is the..."

"LAW," all three shouted at the top of their lungs. The head waiter came running out of the kitchen to see what disaster had befallen his elegant dining room as the siblings sang and danced out the door.

The Dotoshay's arrived twenty minutes early for the show at the Golden Gate Theater. Norm had purchased the $125 tickets as soon as he found out which day his brother and sister were moving to California. Their father, Theo Dotoshay, had directed at their community theater and the year he did "Fiddler on the Roof." Norm, Chris, and Sarah had been in the show and their mother had designed the lights. The production at the Golden Gate was spectacular and they all agreed the actor playing Teveya was the best they had ever seen.

On the way home, Norm decided to see how fast his new Beemer would go. Halfway back to San Jose, he discovered that at least one highway patrolman had no interest in splurch.com stock options.

HARD TO DO

Sunday * April 23, 2000
10:39 AM

"Be strong. Be strong. Be strong," Holly chanted as she walked down Fulton towards the Starbucks where she had agreed to meet Phil for coffee.

"Hey beautiful. Going my way?"

Holly turned. Phil's flaming red Corvette was heading down the hill matching her pace. He smiled and waved.

"Hop in."

"For half a block? " Holly continued to walk down the hill. "I'll meet you in Starbucks."

Phil continued to match her pace. "The Starbucks right there?"

"Duhhhhh," Holly said as she tapped her head with her index finger. "Do you see any other Starbucks in the vicinity?"

A line of cars started piling up behind Phil. "There has to be one or two not very far from here. It's Starbucks. Starbucks are everywhere."

A car started honking. "You are creating a traffic hazard," said Holly as they arrived at the intersection of Fulton and Masonic.

"If you would get in the car, there would be no traffic problem," said Phil as he stopped beside her even though the light was green and the chorus of horns behind him were growing in volume and intensity.

"We are meeting in the Starbucks across the street. Why would I get in your car to ride there?"

"Because...ahhhh...let me see...why would you do that?" Phil pondered the question as the cars behind him became more impatient. "I have to go park and I don't want to park alone. How's that?"

The Range Rover behind Phil pulled out and tried to cross Masonic before the yellow light turned red. SQUEAL. BANG. Fender bender.

Phil got out and gave both drivers, the middle aged black woman in the Rover and an older Italian man in the Ford Taurus, his business card and said to send him the repair bills.

Fifteen minutes later, Holly was sitting in the Starbucks, half way through her Coffee Grande, and Phil walked in.

"Why didn't you let me buy that coffee for you?" he asked sitting across from her.

"I had an immediate caffeine need."

"Let me guess," Phil leaned back in his chair. "You used the three weeks I was in Russia to seriously think about our relationship and have realized that marrying me would be the best idea in the world."

"Actually..."

"Hey Phil!" Two couples in matching sweatsuits and carrying Prince tennis rackets surrounded their table. "What are doing here?" asked the tall man in blue.

"Having coffee with my girlfriend, Holly."

"Girlfriend?" said the blonde woman in pink.

"It's about time Phil got a good woman to take care of him," said the brunette in powder blue.

"That's for sure," laughed the portly man in red.

Phil introduced Holly to the four players and explained how they had all met at Stanford and had since invested in a number of projects together. Holly shook hands, and immediately forgot all their names. The couples had just gone to Mass at Saint Ignatious Church and were now headed to a doubles tournament at the Olympic Club.

As soon as they left, Phil said, "I think we should have a reggae band at the reception."

"There is not going to be a reception."

"Good thinking. We'll just walk from the alter to the limo, go straight to the plane, and fly to our honeymoon."

"We aren't getting married."

"Not now but..."

"Not ever. I told you I would think about it while you were gone and I did. I thought about it every day. I don't want to marry you Phil."

Phil stared at her. "Because I am Jewish?"

"That has nothing to do with it."

"Then why?"

"No spark. No bells. I don't know. It's just not there for me."

Phil sighed and said, "How can it be so the opposite for me? An inferno roars every time I see you and the bells never stop ringing."

"I am sorry."

They sat in silence for almost five minutes and finally Phil said, "You still want to go to the Webby Awards with me?"

"I don't think we should see each other for awhile. It would be too hard."

"Cold turkey?"

"I think that's the only way."

Phil stood up and shook her hand. "Hasta La Vista Baby."

Holly pulled Phil to her and kissed him on the lips. She hugged him, and whispered in his ear, "Thanks Phil. I really like you. I am sorry this didn't work out."

Holly watched out the Starbucks' window as Phil walked up Masonic towards his vintage Corvette. He didn't look back. Not once. She sighed and wondered if she had just made the biggest mistake of her life.

ARM TWISTING

$

Wednesday * April 26, 2000
7:12 AM

Tom was on a mission. The next splurch.com Board of Directors meeting was in two days and he was now doing a "one on one" with every Board member to make sure the meeting went exactly the way he wanted it to go.

TARGET ONE: CLARY WATHERS III
LOCATION: SAN FRANCISCO TENNIS CLUB
TYPE: CASUAL ENCOUNTER
TIME: 7:12 AM

"Hey Tom. Haven't seen you in awhile. I thought you gave up on tennis."

"Hard game to give up." Tom clicked his racket on the edge of the metal table in the lounge overlooking the club's indoor sea of tennis courts. "You coming to the board meeting this Friday?"

"I'll be there if you'll explain how we're going to get that splurch.com stock price back up to some kind of acceptable level."

"Already working on it."

"I checked the price this morning and it hasn't climbed one penny."

"It will any day now. We just started a monster television promotion. Have you seen the commercial yet?"

"Don't watch much television."

"But most of America does."

"That's for sure."

TARGET TWO: HORACE KRENNAN
LOCATION: FAIRMONT HOTEL LOBBY
TYPE: CASUAL ENCOUNTER
TIME: 11:31 AM

"You stalking me again, Samoley."

"Why else would I hang around the lobby waiting for you to go to lunch - which you do at exactly 11:30 every day."

"Saw the commercial."

"And?"

"Sucks."

"Why do you say that?" laughed Tom.

"Didn't make any sense."

"Maybe to an old fart like you. Maybe not for the young adult demographic it's aimed at."

"You want the board to agree to spend all the money we got in the bank to run that one stupid spot on every channel on the dial?"

"We're already in pre-production on a second commercial featuring Staner Lipton."

"At least he's a computer guy. What the hell does Don Johnson know about web sites?"

TARGET THREE: JERRY TENTHER
LOCATION: PLUMED HORSE RESTAURANT
TYPE: DINNER
TIME: 6:41 PM

"How will the television campaign get our stock price back up?"

"Image. Branding. We're creating a name that people are comfortable with," said Tom as he took another bite of his Caesar Salad. "Did you know that we've doubled our unique hits per day since we started our splurch.com television advertising campaign?"

"That has nothing to do with the stock price," Jerry said as he dabbed the corner of his mouth with the monogrammed linen napkin. "If NASDAQ doesn't recover our stockholders are screwed."

"It'll bounce back," said Tom, "it always does. We're just in another cycle. In a couple of months, tech stocks will be higher than they've ever been and the buying frenzy will be on again."

"I hope so."

"Jerry, you've been in this business forever. You know how cyclic it is."

"But there's short cycles and long cycles. What if this an extremely long down turn?"

"Not a chance. This is the new economy. We are headed for fifty years of prosperity."

"If you're wrong there's going to be a lot of unhappy stockholders."

TARGET FOUR: HERNANDO FORMENTO
LOCATION: EL RIO
TYPE: DRINKS
TIME: 9:37 PM

"This round is on me."

"If you insist," said Hernando as he drained his MacAllan Scotch and took another drag on his cigar. "I'll support your television stuff but what are we going to do about the damn site going down every five minutes."

"I've identified the problem. His name is Norm. His splurch.com employment days are almost over."

"Good to hear."

TARGET FIVE: STANER LIPTON
LOCATION: DANCE-A-THON
TYPE: CASUAL ENCOUNTER
TIME: 11:58 PM

"Holy Shit. What's an old man like you doing here?"

"Give me a break Staner," Tom said as he playfully punched the celebrity in the stomach. "Even an old man like me has to go and kick up his heels every once in awhile."

"Saw the television commercial. It's bad."

"I know. We're making another one and we're hoping you'll be in it."

"Staner loves the camera and the camera loves Staner."

"So you'll do it?"

"Sure. But I have to warn ya. I have to approve all the copy."

"No problem."

"And it's gonna cost. This is not a cheap mug."

"You're on the board. Doesn't that get us a price break."

"My agent doesn't believe in price breaks."

"Show biz?"

"Yeah."

"We're going to be talking about the new spot at the Board meeting on Friday. It would be great if you could be there."

"I wasn't planning on it, but if it will help convince those bozos that Staner Lipton is the man to sell splurch.com to the American public - I'll show up."

"Great."

April 29, 2000

Ellison Eclipses Gates in Stock

REVIEW

Monday * May 1, 2000
9:41 AM

Milena looked at the name on her list. NORMAN DOTOSHAY. She turned to Tom and asked. "Ready to do this?"

"Ready, willing, and able," said Tom as he spun around in the conference room chair. "Bring 'em on."

"HOLLY," Milena called. The door opened and Holly's smiling face appeared. "Could you ask Norm to step in please?"

"Will do."

Norm walked in grinning from ear to ear. "You don't have to double my salary. I'll just take a pile of options at six and my brother and sister are here right now. They are settled, and ready to help us build the splurch.com empire."

"We have some bad news Norm," Milena said softly.

Norm stopped smiling and sat in the chair on the other side of the table from Milena and Tom. "What kind of bad news?"

"We have to let you go," said Tom.

"What?"

"Not our decision. It was a Board decision."

"What are you talking about?"

"The site went down too many times. They demanded we do something about it," said Milena.

"It's our NT servers and software. I told you we were going to have problems," Norm swung from Milena to Tom, "You told me we had to save money. You said we would upgrade after the IPO."

213

splurch.com

"You were the man at the switch when the site failed all those days in a row," said Tom.

"But it wasn't MY FAULT!"

"I am sorry Norm," said Milena. She pushed a form across the table towards him. "We'd like you to sign this. It says that you won't sue us or reveal any splurch.com technology to our competitors. You sign and you'll get three months severance pay and full medical and dental for six months."

Norm stared at the form. "Tell me what I can do to keep my job."

The room was silent. Tom finally spoke. "It's a done deal. Sorry."

"This is not happening," Norm whispered.

"You still have an awful lot of options," said Tom.

"Everything I have is underwater," said Norm mechanically. "I'd lose money if I exercised those options today."

"Temporary problem," said Tom. "In a month the price will be back above fifty and you'll be rich again. You can count on it."

"Thank you Norm," Milena said in her "meeting over" tone.

Norm took the form. There were tears in his eyes as he stood up and left the room. Milena looked at the next name on her list - SALVIDOR ZALDIVAR.

Sal came into the room, and asked why Norm was sobbing in his cubicle.

"We had to let him go," said Milena.

"It was a Board decision," said Tom.

"Am I getting fired too?" asked Sal.

"The exact opposite." Tom stood up, came around the table, and put his hand on Sal's shoulder. "We want you to be the new Norm."

Sal stared at the hand on his shoulder and then at the two splurch.com executives. "What if I don't want to be the new Norm?"

Tom removed his hand. "I guess that's your decision but before you give us an answer I want you to think about it very seriously."

"You'll get a large salary increase," said Milena.

"And we'll double your options," added Tom.

"Can I tell you tomorrow?" asked Sal.

"Sure," said Tom expansively.

"We need an answer by noon," said Milena curtly.

"My insurance thing is still screwed up you know."

"What insurance thing?" asked Tom.

"Sal's bills haven't been paid yet," said Milena. "Did you call that number I gave you?"

"I tried. It's always busy."

"Don't worry Sal," said Tom. "You're an important guy. We'll take care of you."

By the end of the day, Tom and Milena had talked with every member of the splurch.com team and asked Holly to sit in the "hot seat."

"You are doing a great job," Milena said.

"Yes I am," said Holly. "But enough about me. Why did Norm get fired?"

"Board decision," said Tom.

Milena quickly changed the topic. "We want to ask something a little strange."

"You've been going out with Phil Steinberg?" said Tom.

"Yes, but..."

"His company would be a perfect fit with splurch.com," said Tom. "We'd like you to introduce us to him. Maybe Milena and I could take you and Phil out to dinner."

Holly started laughing and couldn't stop. Eventually she explained how she had just broken up with Phil. Tom said to make sure that she let him know if things changed and then raced out the door forty minutes late for a dinner date with another potential Mrs. Tom Samoley.

Milena joked with Holly for a few minutes and then spent an hour planning a strategic partner presentation and another two hours responding to her e-mail. On the way home, she picked up a Veggie Sub at Subway and rented the movie "Sixth Sense" at Blockbuster.

When she got to her condo, Milena stretched out on the four poster bed to eat supper and watch the film. She finished most of the sub but was fast asleep long before the "Sixth Sense" surprise ending.

May 1, 2000

Top Companies Have Great Year

SPLURCH STOCK

5/1/00 - 9/1/00

May 5, 2000 SPRC @ $17.45
Norm is hired at alwayscredit.com.

May 8, 2000 SPRC @ $25.17
Staner Lipton argues with **Tom** about the stupid lines in the new splurch.com commercial. Tom decides to perform the spot himself.

May 13, 2000 SPRC @ $36.47
Sal scores the winning goal in his first game back to ultimate frisbee. **Gersta**, his Everquest partner, drives up from San Mateo to cheer him on.

May 22, 2000 SPRC @ $70.19
Sarah Dotoshay starts work at The Tech. **Chris Dotoshay** is hired by **Norm** to do freelance programming for alwayscredit.com.

May 29, 2000 SPRC @ $61.45
Tom orders **Milena** to double the television buy for his new television commercial.

June 1, 2000 SPRC @ $88.45
Splurch.com moves to San Jose. **Sal** and **Holly** help with the move but tell **Milena** they're leaving splurch.com instead of San Francisco.

June 9, 2000 SPRC @ $108.45
Milena flys to Florida for a week vacation with her mom.

June 11, 2000 SPRC @ $103.14
The splurch.com web site goes down.

June 14, 2000 SPRC @ $81.67
Splurch.com is down for 72 hours. **Milena** flys back on the red eye.

June 17, 2000 SPRC @ $76.32
Holly goes to San Francisco Symphony's "American Mavericks" festival with **Phil Steinberg**

217

splurch.com

July 1, 2000 SPRC @ $55.12
Holly and **Sal** get a great deal on a two bedroom apartment.. **Norm**, **Beth**, and **Chris Dotoshay** help the two friends move in together.

July 14, 2000 SPRC @ $43.15
Tom orders **Milena** to reduce the "burn rate" by firing half the splurch.com employees

July 18, 2000 SPRC @ $36.39
Splurch.com server farm has power outage. Splurch.com goes off-line.

July 19, 2000 SPRC @ $27.02
Servers still down. Splurch.com has been off-line for 24 hours.

July 23, 2000 SPRC @ $22.45
Splurch.com still off-line. **Tom** calls an emergency meeting of the splurch.com **Board of Directors**. No one shows up.

July 25, 2000 SPRC @ $16.17
Splurch has less than 5 million dollars in the bank. **Tom** orders **Milena** to fire all "non-essential" employees.

July 28, 2000 SPRC @ $11.45
Milena spends weekend in Tahoe with **Addy** and doesn't bring her cell.

July 31, 2000 SPRC @ $9.96
Tom fires **Milena** in the morning and rehires her in the afternoon.

August 14, 2000 SPRC @ $7.24
Alwayscredit.com declares bankruptcy. **Norm** informs the IRS and starts looking for another job.

August 18, 2000 SPRC @ $6.67
The *Wall Street Journal* runs an article on patent infringement and infers splurch.com stole all their technology.

August 23, 2000 SPRC @ $1.13
Tom tries to sell splurch.com. He can find no takers.

September 1, 2000 SPRC @ $.39
Splurch.com closes its doors.

PINK SLIP PARTY

Thursday * March 29, 2001
6:37 PM

Milena picks up her drink and turns. She is immediately looking into two familiar smiling brown eyes.

"Holly, what are you doing here?"

"I am a red badge employment seeker?"

"I thought you were working at that dot com on Folsom that was doing so great."

"WAS doing great," explains Holly as she follows Milena towards the back of Holy Cow. "Full speed ahead until last Friday when the CEO announced we had an hour to pack our personal stuff because the repossession company was on the way."

"No warning?"

"Zero, Zip, Zilch."

"Sounds familiar," Milena points out two empty chairs in the middle of the boisterous pink slip party.

"Was that what it was like when splurch.com shut down?" Holly asks as she flops in a chair.

"If you and Sal hadn't deserted us, you would have seen for yourself."

"Oh dang," Holly says as she puts both hands on her cheeks in a Home Alone impression. "I didn't see the death of a dream. How could I miss such a golden opportunity?"

"It wasn't that bad," says Milena as she puts her drink on a table covered with carvings and cigarette burns. "Only Tom and I were left and we both knew exactly what day the money would run out."

"SO, if Sal and I had moved to San Jose with you, we wouldn't

219

have been around when you guys shut the doors anyway."

"Probably not," sighs Milena and quickly changes the subject to stop the visions of those last traumatic days from flooding her brain. "You and Sal still living together?"

"Happy apartment-mates we be."

"No romance."

"Just friends - still."

"What about the boy billionaire?"

"Phil?"

"Heard you went to the Webby Awards together."

"Big mistake. After that night filled with dot com self congratulations, Phil called me every day for a month."

"You're giving up a guaranteed financial future."

"A future filled with insanity," says Holly. "I think Phil might be getting over it though. I heard he changed the name of his boat."

"No longer the Holly Dream?"

"Now the Happy Dream."

"He only had to re-paint three letters," laughs Milena.

"That's probably why he's rich and I will never be," Holly says chewing on her ice cubes. "I would have re-painted all the letters."

"I am assuming Sal is still gainfully employed?"

"Of course. Mr. Can Do Everything is working for a video game company in San Rafael and loving it. He's a man born to make video games."

"And the video game business isn't going away."

"That's for sure."

"But Sal can't ride his beloved bike to work."

"Yes he can. He just has to leave long before I start thinking about my morning caffeine fix."

The two former splurch.com workers watch the frantic networking around them. Blue badges are employers. Red badges are employment seekers. Green badges are media and observers. Lots of Red and Green. Very few Blue.

"I've been thinking about Norm," Milena finally says. "Do you know what happened to him?"

"I talk to him on the phone every couple of weeks."

"Really?"

"I called him the night you booted him off the Splurch team."

"Why didn't you tell me that?"

"He asked me not to."

"Did he get a job right away?"

"Immediately. The tech world was still cooking a year ago. A week later he was working at alwayscredit.com for more money than he was getting from splurch.com."

"His brother and sister?"

"Loving California dreaming. Both got jobs are still bunking with Norm."

"Is Norm still at alwayscredit?"

"Of course not.. It folded about the same time as splurch.com.. But he's more careful with his money now and made a deal with the IRS so he can keep his house and eat regularly."

"Where's he working now?"

"At the University of San Francisco."

"Isn't that where you went to school?"

"The Head of the Technology Department is my friend," says Holly doing a cheerleader dance with her hands. "Go Holly Go."

"THERE you are," a male voice cuts through the raucous crowd, "interviewing one of our former employees."

Tom Samoley was suddenly standing in front of them. "Hey Molly how are you doing?"

"It's Holly," says Milena quickly.

"Oops," says Tom. "Sorry Holly. It's been awhile. Has Milena hired you yet?"

"Tom stop," Milena says glancing up at Tom's smiling face, "I haven't agreed to leave my stable marketing job at HP."

"You will," laughs Tom. "It's streaming media. It's the future. We're going to double my Dad's video distribution business in six months."

"I don't know."

"You want to work for us, don't you Holly?"

"I have a red tag on my chest don't I?"

"Holly's in," says Tom as he grabbed another chair and sat down. "That means you're in too, right Milena?"

Milena looks at the grinning venture capitalist and then at the laughing cheerleader.

"I suppose," she groans. "I suppose I'm in."

thanks

Rick Alber
Steve Baker
Kimberly Baldwin
Michael Baldwin
Paul Bergmann
MJ Bogatin
Nell Bostwick
Eli Brown
George Clark
Dan Coffey
Steve Cox
Smiley Curtis
Patrick Flaherty
Peter Garrity
Tricia Gray
Hilda Hughes
Genny Hutchison
Dylan Jones
Howard Karp
Merle Kessler
Leon Martell
Robb New
Sophie Ortiz
Brooks Oswald
Dave Pangaro
Ed Rachles
Michael Robertson
Charles Rudnick
Ed Santa Ana
Eric Scheide
Bob Steinberg
Mary Swanson
David Tetzlaff
Tony Tiano
Jim Turner
Ron Turner
Siamak Vossoughi

Photo: Matt Allard

Bill Allard is a writer, director, performer, and producer. He is a founding member of the comedy troupe Duck's Breath Mystery Theater and lives in San Francisco with his wife, Margaret, and his sons, Richard and Matthew.

Bill plays basketball whenever he can.